"I wasn't interfering with anything and I don't need your protection. I'm not afraid."

Still, Helena laid her phone down on the table in front of Hunter. "I don't expect the killer to contact me."

"Good. Neither do I."

"And I'm not planning to go looking for trouble."

"Also good because I'd hate to put you under house arrest."

"On what grounds?"

"I'll think of something."

He was surely bluffing. When he finished with the phone, she walked him to the door.

Instead of leaving, he held the door open and looked down at her, his gaze burning into hers. He leaned closer until his lips were only inches away from her mouth.

Old urges erupted inside her, a hunger that she'd thought was lost forever.

"Stay safe, Helena," he murmured. And then he turned and was gone.

NEW ORLEANS NOIR

JOANNA WAYNE

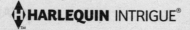

HARLEQUIN INTRIGUE®

To everyone who loves a south Louisiana mystery. To my great friends who live there and to everyone who has ever longed to visit New Orleans.

ISBN-13: 978-1-335-60456-9

New Orleans Noir

Copyright © 2019 by Jo Ann Vest

Recycling programs for this product may not exist in your area.

This edition published by arrangement with Harlequin Books S.A.

For questions and comments about the quality of this book, please contact us at CustomerService@Harlequin.com.

Printed in U.S.A.

www.Harlequin.com

Joanna Wayne began her professional writing career in 1994. Now, more than fifty published books later, Joanna has gained a worldwide following with her cutting-edge romantic suspense and Texas family series, such as Sons of Troy Ledger and Big "D" Dads. Joanna currently resides in a small community north of Houston, Texas, with her husband. You may write Joanna at PO Box 852, Montgomery, TX 77356, or connect with her at joannawayne.com.

Books by Joanna Wayne

Harlequin Intrigue

New Orleans Noir

The Kavanaughs

Riding Shotgun
Quick-Draw Cowboy
Fearless Gunfighter
Dropping the Hammer

Big "D" Dads: The Daltons

Trumped Up Charges
Unrepentant Cowboy
Hard Ride to Dry Gulch
Midnight Rider
Showdown at Shadow Junction
Ambush at Dry Gulch

Sons of Troy Ledger

Cowboy Swagger
Genuine Cowboy
AK-Cowboy
Cowboy Fever
Cowboy Conspiracy

Big "D" Dads

Son of a Gun
Live Ammo
Big Shot

Visit the Author Profile page at Harlequin.com.

CAST OF CHARACTERS

Helena Cosworth—An up-and-coming artist returning to New Orleans to sell her beloved late grandmother's historic carriage house and the four apartments surrounding the courtyard.

Hunter Bergeron—A homicide detective determined to keep Helena safe and to arrest a serial killer before he strikes again.

Mia Cosworth—Helena's grandmother who had contact with the killer days before she died from a fall.

Ella Grayson—One of Mia Cosworth's tenants whose great niece Elizabeth was the most recent victim of the serial killer.

Alyssa Orillon—A friend of Helena's and a self-admitted fake psychic who works in the French Quarter.

Cory Barker—An important member of the serial killer task force, which is supervised by Hunter.

Eulalie—Cory Barker's mother, who owns a B and B and swamp-tour business near where Elizabeth Grayson was killed.

Antoine Robicheaux—A former FBI forensics expert who is volunteering with the task force.

Pierre Benoit and Connor Harrington—Tenants living in apartments on the carriage house property.

Lacy Blankenship—A tourist in the French Quarter who bears an amazing resemblance to Elizabeth Grayson, the serial killer's most recent victim.

Prologue

Elizabeth Grayson jerked forward as the car skidded to a slippery stop. The deserted dirt road that had been barely passable before had suddenly disappeared, replaced by clumps of tall grass, deeper pockets of brown water and what appeared to be a wide stretch of swampland.

Her nerves grew edgy. "Where are we?"

"Somewhere we can finally be totally alone." He flicked off the headlights.

"It's pitch-black out here," she murmured.

"Are you afraid of the dark or of being alone with me?" he teased, his voice deep and sexy, *almost* melting her anxious vibes.

"I'm never afraid when I'm with you."

"That's what I like to hear, baby. You always know how to please me."

She loved the way he talked to her, as if she were his equal though he was older and much more mature than the high school boys she'd dated back home. The sloppy kisses of teenage boys never thrilled her the way his did. She'd never melted at their touch.

He killed the motor, then stretched his arm across the back of the seat and slipped it around her shoulders. "This is a favorite place of mine when I need to get away," he said.

"Really? It seems so isolated."

"I see it as private and a little forbidden," he said, "but if it makes you nervous, I can drive back into town."

"No. I don't want to go back," she answered quickly.

All she'd been able to think about for the past two days was seeing him again. She craved his touch and the way her body came alive when he slid his hands beneath her blouse or when he slipped his tongue inside her mouth.

Unfortunately, their making out had been limited to what they could manage in the back seat of his sports car parked behind a sleazy bar in a part of town she hadn't known existed until a few nights ago. Even then she'd wanted more, but he'd held back. He'd wanted to wait until everything was right.

They'd met last Saturday night when Elizabeth had been out with a girlfriend who lived in Metairie. Her friend Melinda had managed to snare fake IDs for both of them before Elizabeth had flown to New Orleans to visit her great-aunt for spring break.

Melinda had already been tipsy by the time Elizabeth noticed the hunk of a man staring at her. He nodded when they made eye contact but didn't approach them. When he smiled and left the bar, she followed him outside.

One hello in his deep, sexy voice and she was certain he was the most gorgeous and exciting man she'd ever met. She'd whispered her phone number into his ear as he opened the door to his black sports car.

He'd called the very next day. She'd thought of nothing but him since then.

He wasn't driving the sports car tonight, but a mud-encrusted pickup truck more suitable for the terrain. He pulled a flashlight from the truck's console and flicked it on as he climbed from behind the wheel. He reached behind the driver's seat and picked up what appeared to be a blanket.

Her pulse went crazy. Spring break was almost over. She'd be flying back to Tulsa on Sunday and might never see him again. Her heart would surely break but how much worse would it be if she didn't have this time with him tonight to treasure?

Complete privacy. And a blanket. They were surely going to make love. It would be the first time for her to go all the way. He would be experienced. He'd teach her all she needed to know.

He walked around the truck, opened her door and took her hand. She quivered in anticipation, ready for this in every way.

Aunt Ella still thought of Elizabeth as a kid and constantly warned her to be careful. As much as Elizabeth had hated lying to her tonight, she'd had no choice.

If her great-aunt could see her now, she'd be horrified. She would tell Elizabeth she was tempting disaster. The thought intensified Helena's anxiety.

"Okay. I can tell you're not ready," he said, dropping her hand. "I obviously misread the signs."

"You didn't," she assured him. "There's nowhere I'd rather be than here with you." That much was true.

Taking a deep, steadying breath, she stepped out of the truck. The earth was damp, sucking like quicksand. The grass was almost to her knees, hiding anything that might be crawling beneath it. Like snakes. Or tarantulas.

He put a thumb beneath her chin and nudged until she faced him. He leaned over and his lips met hers. Desire pummeled her as heated juices seeped into the silky red panties she'd worn just for him.

She'd be a fool to do anything to spoil this moment. He wasn't the man of her dreams. She'd never had dreams this good.

They walked for ten minutes or more, dodging spreading palmetto fronds, clumps of reeds and the exposed roots of cypress trees until they reached the slippery bank of a murky bayou.

The moon finally peeked from behind the clouds, providing enough illumination that he turned off the flashlight. A few yards farther and he took a different path, not stopping until they reached a slightly higher and dryer area. He dropped her hand and her insides quaked as he spread the blanket.

He kicked out of his shoes and lay down on his side, his right elbow supporting him so that he could meet her gaze. He opened his arms for her to join him.

She hesitated and scanned the area one last time. "Are you sure there are no snakes or alligators around here?" she asked.

"I guarantee you that before this night is over, you won't be worried at all about snakes, alligators or any other creatures of the swamp. Now undress slowly so I can watch," he said, an authoritative bent to his voice that hadn't been there before. By the time she was totally naked, passion enflamed her.

She lay down beside him, anticipating heaven.

Instead she fell into the depths of hell.

Chapter One

Helena Cosworth gathered her luggage from the taxi and walked the short distance to an intricately designed seven-foot-high metal gate. She stood there for a moment, letting the familiarity seep into her tired bones until grief-crinkled memories invaded and dampened her spirit.

The historic French Quarter carriage house just beyond the gate had been her second home for as long as she could remember. Her mother had died when she was only five.

Her dad had been an oil and gas executive who went wherever he was needed. If the location wasn't right for raising a daughter, she went to boarding schools in the States. Even when she lived with him, she spent most summers and many holidays in New Orleans with her energetic, fun-loving grandmother Mia.

During those visits, Mia had made her the center of her life and the adventure-laden Crescent City was their playground. The zoo, Audubon Park, the bustling Mississippi River, theater, trips down St. Charles Avenue on the cable car, parades galore. And the many hours spent in museums nurturing Helena's passion for art.

The lifestyle wasn't ideal by everyone's standards, but it worked for them. When her father had died from a sudden heart attack a week before her high school graduation, she moved in with Mia and began her college career the following fall at Tulane University.

Helena reached to the keypad and punched in the code for the security system Mia had installed a few years back. A twist of the handle and a firm shove and the gate squeaked open.

Heat and humidity hit like a wave of steam as she stepped inside the courtyard where the day's fetid air seemed trapped by the surrounding walls. She was quickly revived by the fragrance of night jasmine that overflowed from a huge pot and the cooling mist from the impressive angel fountain in the middle of the spacious area.

She didn't even glance toward the four apartments surrounding the rest of the courtyard as she made her way to the bright red door that served as the main entrance to the carriage house. The original, barn-style doors on the front of the house that had once swung open for horses and carriages had been replaced with brick walls and fake, shuttered windows years ago.

A shudder of emptiness shook Helena's resolve not to fall into a state of teary-eyed depression. It had been just over five weeks since she'd received the heart-breaking news of Mia's tragic accident, and although she'd been here for the funeral, the wound of grief felt fresh.

She opened the door and stepped into the marble foyer. The air conditioner was blasting away. Thankfully, she'd let Ella Grayson know when she was arriving. Ella had been one of Mia's tenants for years and she and Mia had been fast friends. They'd become closer than ever after Ella's great-niece, Elizabeth, had been brutally murdered last spring.

Helena parked her luggage by the door and dropped her handbag onto the antique cherrywood table before flicking on the delicate Tiffany lamp. Illumination climbed the foyer walls in enchanting patterns. Everything looked the same as it had when Mia was alive. Even the citrusy fragrance of the candles she'd burned nightly lingered in the air.

The property now belonged to Helena—at least until she found a buyer. Giving up the old carriage house would be like giving away a chunk of her soul, but her career was in Boston. She would start her new job with one of the most successful individually owned art galleries in the city on November 1. A few of her paintings already hung in the gallery.

Helena traipsed across the cozy sitting room with its worn Persian rug, comfortable furniture and shelves filled with books and framed photographs.

When she stepped into the kitchen, memories attacked full force. She'd had morning coffee at the small, round mahogany table with Mia for as long as she could remember, though when she was young, Helena's cup was filled mostly with cold milk and a shot of honey.

They'd sipped the chicory-laden brew from dainty flowered cups while Mia filled Helena's young head with simple answers to life's mysteries.

Like why king cakes had plastic babies hidden inside them and why people riding floats at Mardi Gras always wore masks. And why even rich people ate po'boy sandwiches that needed to be dressed.

Heart aching, Helena finally walked to the foot of the elegant, curved staircase. The staircase where her grandmother had slipped and fallen to her death.

According to the medical examiner, a severe brain trauma caused by the fall had likely killed her within minutes. Minutes that she'd been totally alone.

Helena forced herself to go on, climbing the stairs slowly, stopping only a few seconds at the landing before making it to the second floor and the bedroom she'd always thought of as her own.

A pale orchid coverlet and countless pillows covered the four-poster bed. Beyond that, tall French doors opened onto a balcony that overlooked Dumaine Street.

Helena unlatched the doors, swung them open and stepped onto the balcony.

Spicy odors of fried seafood wafted through the air and suddenly Helena was starved. She hadn't eaten since breakfast and that was only her usual yogurt and granola. It was nearly seven now.

There would be time for memories and unpacking later. A beer and a po'boy were calling her name.

Chapter Two

Alyssa Orillon rinsed her empty teacup and placed it on the countertop to be carried upstairs to her main living quarters later. The small downstairs kitchen was barely big enough for the mini-fridge, a microwave, a card table and two padded wooden chairs she'd picked up for next to nothing in a used furniture store on Magazine Street.

The remaining five hundred square feet of the home's ground floor was dedicated to her cozy waiting room and a private counseling area. Located only two blocks from Jackson Square, she was right in the thick of the tourist pedestrian traffic, though business was slow tonight.

Not untypical for a Tuesday night. Last weekend's convention goers had gone home. This week's hadn't arrived yet.

She glanced at her watch. Half past eight. Too early to call it a night—especially since she didn't open her doors until early afternoon on weekdays.

Inconveniently, the beginning of a headache was tapping at her right temple. An uneasy feeling had been messing with her nerves all afternoon, the kind of vague sense of anxiety one might expect from a psychic—unless said psychic was a complete and total fraud—like Alyssa.

Fake, but not a rip-off artist, as some of her competitors were. Alyssa was an expert at giving customers what they wanted. Most people were fairly easy to read if you honed your skills as well as Alyssa had.

The professionally printed sign painted on her door lured in the type of customers she handled best.

Alyssa Orillon—Psychic.
Is true love in your future?
Is the man in your life right for you?
Is something wonderful about to bless your life?
The answers you desire are waiting inside.

The sparkling, crystal ball rotating in the large front window provided an additional enticement for the curious or extrasensory believer. The crimson velvet drape behind the ball blocked the view of the studio's dimly lit interior, making it even more mysterious.

Unlike Alyssa, her grandmother Brigitte had the gift in spades. At least she had until she claimed old age weakened her powers. Before moving into an assisted living center in Covington, Brigitte had frequently told Alyssa how lucky she was not to be constantly haunted by other people's nightmares.

Alyssa walked to the window, notched back the heavy drape and peeked out. Things were getting livelier on the street. A few more drinks and hopefully someone would knock on her door, enter her chambers and cross her palms with cash.

The only person she recognized was Andy, the scruffy young man at the curb playing his sax for tips. A nice guy, but bad luck found him at every turn. Good tippers didn't.

Just as she started to let go of the curtain's edge, she spotted another familiar figure. Hunter Bergeron. Tall, ruggedly handsome, with dark brown hair that always looked mussed. Alyssa suspected there were plenty of young women who'd love to run their hands through it and straighten it for him.

Had she been a decade or so younger, she might have been one of those women.

Hunter was low-key for a hard-nosed homicide detective. He could push when he had to, though. He'd proved that when questioning half the people in the French Quarter after Elizabeth Grayson's murder.

She walked over, opened her door and tried to get his attention, just to say hello and perhaps pick his brain for a minute about the serial killer investigation. He didn't look up, his attention focused on a stunning young woman in a bright yellow sundress, who didn't appear to see him watching.

The young woman leaned over and dropped a bill into the musician's open sax case. When she straightened, she turned Alyssa's way.

Oh my God. That is Mia Cosworth's granddaughter. She had no idea Helena was back in town.

Alyssa stepped outside, waving frantically until she got Helena's attention. Helena smiled and began to maneuver her way around a cluster of tourists.

Seconds later, Helena stepped through the open door and threw her arms around Alyssa in the same enthusiastic way she had when Helena had been a kid and her grandmother would bring her to visit.

Good memories until…

Alyssa trembled. She pulled away from Helena and reached for the back of one of the waiting room chairs for balance.

"What's wrong?" Helena asked.

"It's this dreaded headache," Alyssa lied. "I've been fighting it all day. I just need to sit down."

Helena helped her into the chair. "Can I get you something for it?"

"If you don't mind. There's a bottle of aspirin on the table in the small kitchen and a pitcher of cold water in the fridge." This was far more than a headache, but she needed time alone to regain her equilibrium.

She leaned back and closed her eyes. It didn't help. Instead weird images popped into her head as if she were hallucinating. She'd experienced this before but not in years and not often.

The harder she tried to force the images from her mind, the more vivid they became. It was Helena being chased by a man who was too blurry to identify. And blood. Lots of blood, covering Helena's clothes and her hair and part of her face.

This isn't real. I'm not an authentic medium. This is some nightmarish trick my mind is playing on me.

But why now?

The images faded as fast as they'd come. Alyssa

shuddered, determined to ignore the cold horror that rode her spine, and pulled herself together. She could not plant her groundless, horrifying hallucinations into Helena's mind.

Chapter Three

Helena shook two aspirin from the bottle into Alyssa's palm and then handed her a glass of cold water. Alyssa was no longer shaking the way she had been, but she didn't look well.

"Should I call 911?" Helena asked. "Just in case you're coming down with something." Or was having a stroke—or worse.

"No. No doctors. No ambulance. I was dizzy for a minute, but I'm fine now."

"You don't look fine. You look as if you saw a ghost."

"No chance of that. I couldn't conjure one up if I tried. Believe me, I know."

Her attempt at humor fell flat. "You should at least get checked out at the emergency clinic," Helena said. "I'll be glad to go with you."

"That's totally not necessary, but thanks. What I could really use is some conversation with someone who doesn't expect me to read their mind."

To emphasize her point, Alyssa stood, walked to

the door and flipped the rectangular plaque from Open to Closed.

"Have a seat," Alyssa insisted, "and fill me in on all you've been doing since I saw you last. You cut out so soon after your grandmother's memorial service that I didn't get a chance to properly say goodbye."

"I was in a state of shock," Helena admitted. "Her death was so sudden, so unexpected. I'm not sure what I said to anyone."

"I understand that," Alyssa said. "Her death was a shock to all of us. She was a dynamo those last few months, as driven as I'd ever seen her."

"I know she was busy trying to raise money to offer an award to anyone who helped identify Elizabeth's killer."

"She raised over a hundred thousand dollars. Everyone was amazed."

"Mia could always do anything she set her mind to." Helena settled in the nearest chair. "I didn't realize she raised that much, though."

Alyssa dropped into the facing chair and kicked out of her beaded sandals. She pulled her bare feet into the chair with her, tucking them beneath her long, flowing skirt.

There was no overhead lighting in the reception area, but red silk squares were draped over the shades of a pair of brass, dragon-shaped lamps. Flames flickered from a cluster of fragrant candles that dominated a round table in the center of the space, bathing the room in a warm, sensual glow.

As a small child, Helena had thought Alyssa's home

was as magical as the Greek and Roman gods in Mia's colorfully illustrated books.

By the time she understood what powers a psychic supposedly possessed, she'd outgrown her belief in magic.

"What's going on in the neighborhood?" Helena asked. "Any gossip I should know about?"

"I'll start with the bad and get it out of the way. Fancy died."

"Fancy, the portrait painter?"

"That's the one. She'd set up her paints and easel in that same spot outside Jackson Square every day for as long as I've lived here—and that's more years than I care to admit."

"I credit much of my interest in art to her," Helena said. "When I was five all I wanted for Christmas was an easel and some paints so I could make pictures like Miss Fancy."

"She would have loved that story," Alyssa said.

"I wish I had shared it with her."

"The locals threw her a real New Orleans funeral with a jazz parade and lots of dancing in the streets, similar to what we all did for Mia, except less organization and fewer musicians."

"You guys definitely sent Mia off in style," Helena agreed. They'd left very little of the organization up to her.

Most tourists saw the French Quarter as a hodge-podge of bars, restaurants and souvenir shops. They didn't realize what a diverse group of locals resided beyond the historically correct exteriors.

Mia had fit right in the community and couldn't walk down the street without stopping to talk to half a dozen people and waving to more.

"Any other happenings I should know about?" Helena asked.

"You can order groceries locally now and have them delivered. That's the most exciting new thing we've got going for us. The second most popular topic is the French Kiss Killer and I really don't want to talk about him tonight."

"I'm with you, but I admit facts of the brutal murder still haunt me, perhaps because I'd met Elizabeth several times over the years and was always impressed by her vibrant personality. Or maybe it was just the senselessness of it all."

"Me and my big mouth," Alyssa said. "I said I wasn't going to talk about the murder and then I just throw it right out there."

"It was bound to come up, sooner or later. Elephants in the room never stay unnoticed for long."

"I'm convinced they'll find the killer," Alyssa said. "Hunter Bergeron is heading up the task force and he's not the type of cop to give up until he arrests his man."

Hunter Bergeron. Helena's nerves went edgy. She swallowed hard, angry with herself that she was having any kind of reaction to merely hearing his name. She couldn't keep that up.

It had been six years since he'd broken her heart. She'd moved on. So had he, even doing a tour of duty with the Marines or so Mia had told her.

The memories were still there, but they were buried so deep they no longer had the power to rip her apart.

"I'm so glad we had this visit," Helena said, "but if you're sure you're okay now, I really should go." She stood before Alyssa could drag her into a conversation about Hunter. "We should have lunch together soon."

"I'd like that." Alyssa followed Helena and switched her sign back to Open before she unlatched the door.

"Are you sure you feel like seeing more customers tonight?" Helena asked.

"I'm sure. Besides, the later it gets the drunker they tend to be and the easier it is for them to part with their bucks and believe whatever I tell them."

"No doubt." Helena smiled as she took both Alyssa's hands in hers.

"Be careful," Alyssa murmured. Her words took on an ominous tone.

"I will."

"I don't mean just tonight. I mean all the time. You never know who you can trust these days."

"You're right." Hunter Bergeron had taught her that. She gave Alyssa a quick parting hug and then hit the busy street again.

The music, laughter and smiling faces didn't have their usual uplifting effect. Helena found it hard to shake the talk of the serial killer and the fearful timbre of Alyssa's parting warning.

Could it be that Alyssa was more psychic than she'd ever admitted to Mia?

Helena tried to ignore the plunge in her own spirits as she reached the tall metal gate and punched in Mia's private code.

Once inside the courtyard, the anxiety eased. She was home.

Only Mia was gone forever, and home wasn't home anymore.

HUNTER BERGERON HAD followed Helena at a distance, mesmerized by the sway of her narrow hips. He wasn't the only one noticing her. Almost every man she passed gave her at least a futile glance.

The first time he'd laid eyes on her, he'd thought her the most beautiful girl in the world. She'd changed in the six years since then, wore her hair longer, developed the curves of a woman instead of a young coed.

Tonight, she was so damned stunning she boggled his mind. She was out of his league and had always been. Any hope of rekindling the fire that had once raged between them would end in heartbreak. He didn't need that now.

He leaned against the front of a building across the street from the carriage house, staying deep in the shadows beneath an iron balcony. Several minutes later, the light in the upstairs bedroom flicked on.

He knew that bedroom intimately. His legs felt like rubber as he finally turned and walked away.

But he'd be back. He had no choice. Unknowingly, she might be his only link to the French Kiss Killer.

And that could get her killed.

Chapter Four

Helena jerked awake to the sound of clanking metal garbage cans and the grinding of compactors. She'd closed the airy privacy curtains last night but had failed to close the heavy, noise reducing drapes.

She stretched beneath the crisp, cotton sheet and punched her pillow over her ears. A couple more hours of sleep would provide a much better start to a very busy day. Unfortunately, her mind was already splintering into a dozen different directions.

By the time the streets had become relatively quiet again, she'd given up on sleep. She threw her legs over the side of the bed, tugged her cotton nightshirt down midthigh and shoved her bare feet into a pair of fuzzy flip-flops.

The first thing on her agenda was coffee. The difficult part would be that this morning she'd have it alone.

The antique Swiss grandfather clock on the wide landing struck the hour. The six melodic chimes echoed in the quiet house.

If Mia were still alive, her sweet soprano voice would have wrapped itself around an old hymn or maybe she'd be in a twangy country mood. Her musical tastes ran the gamut.

Cherishing the memories while trying not to let them slide into overpowering grief, Helena forced herself to continue down the stairs and into the kitchen. She flicked on the overhead light and started a pot of coffee.

When it was ready, Helena filled one of the colorful cups she and Mia had purchased in the French Market the last time they'd gone shopping for spring's first Creole tomatoes. So many great yet simple times they'd spent together.

All never to be again. She wondered if the sorrow at being back here would be less intense if Mia's death hadn't come so suddenly—not that she could change that.

Helena took her coffee and walked to what had been Mia's bedroom suite. As always, a pile of books was messily stacked on her bedside table.

Helena padded across the lush crème-colored carpet and picked up the top book. She expected one of the historical romances that her grandmother loved or a nonfiction book dealing with the history of New Orleans.

Instead, it was a study of profiling serial killers in America. Helena scanned the titles of the next three books. All dealt with some aspect of serial killers.

Helena shuddered at the thought of Mia delving into such gore for bedtime reading.

She'd called her grandmother at least once a week

between Elizabeth Grayson's murder and Mia's fatal accident. Mia had assured Helena every time that she was too busy with her fund-raising campaign and attempting to cheer up Ella that there was no time left for her to wallow in gloom and doom.

Her reading material suggested differently.

Helena dropped to the side of the bed and picked up a thick gray hardback book with no dust jacket. Several bookmarks were scattered among the pages.

She opened the tome to the first marked page and her eyes went immediately to a paragraph highlighted in neon yellow.

Serial killers may be physically attractive to the opposite sex and function somewhat successfully in society for long periods of time in between their crimes.

A few paragraphs down on that same page:

It is often difficult to predict the future targets of the killers as they may not understand the involved dynamics themselves.

Below that passage, in her meticulous script, Mia had written one name in the margin.

Hunter Bergeron.

Had Mia been questioning Hunter about what she was reading? If so, when had they become friends?

Helena closed the book but took it with her when she left the room. She'd read more later, but she needed to finish unpacking and then shower and dress before her real estate agent, Randi Lester, arrived.

Be careful whom you trust.

Unexpectedly, Alyssa's warning came back to haunt her as she left the bedroom.

She'd heed the warning, especially when it came to Hunter Bergeron. With any luck she wouldn't run into him at all.

HELENA BUZZED RANDI through the gate at exactly 8:28 for their 8:30 appointment. Nice to know the woman who'd hopefully be listing the carriage house and the four apartments surrounding the rest of the courtyard was prompt.

Helena unlocked the door, stepped outside and watched as Randi crossed the courtyard. The Realtor paused near the fountain and turned a full 360 degrees, taking in the view.

The picture on the business card Randi had mailed her didn't do her justice. She appeared to be approximately the same height as Helena's five feet six, or would have been if her stiletto heels hadn't given her at least a four-inch boost.

In her midthirties, Helena judged, with an athletic build and sun-streaked hair cut into a layered bob. Silver bangles dangled from her ears. A frilly white blouse topped a pair of black-and-white checked ankle pants.

"Impressive," Randi pronounced once she met Helena at the door. "One of the biggest and nicest courtyards I've seen in this part of the French Quarter. It will grab any potential buyer's attention immediately. And nothing beats a great first impression in the real estate business."

"Glad to hear that," Helena said as she extended a hand. "I'm Helena Cosworth."

"I know. I recognized you from your picture on Facebook."

"I sometimes forget I have that public image floating around in digital space. I should probably update it."

"I wouldn't," Randi said. "It's a great likeness even if you do look even younger in person."

"Thanks, but flattery will only get you a cup of coffee or a glass of iced tea," Helena said.

"Iced tea sounds terrific." Randi stepped inside and followed Helena to the kitchen. "It's nice to finally meet you in person, although our many phone conversations and the enthusiastic manner in which Beverly Ingram has described you make me feel as if we've old friends."

"I'd hoped Bev might be with you," Helena said. "I know she's familiar with the rental history of each of the four units as well as the needed repairs and upgrades."

"She'd planned to join us, but she's in Little Rock this morning waiting for the arrival of her first grandbaby. A boy. She left me a spreadsheet showing the rental history for the past five years, so we're good."

"No problem. A new grandson tops a meeting any day."

Helena poured two glasses of iced tea and wrapped them in a cloth napkin to catch the condensation.

She'd met Bev on several occasions while visiting Mia. She owned and operated the French Quarter rental management agency that had handled Mia's four apartments for at least the last decade. Bev had recommended Randi when Helena mentioned selling the house.

"Would you like a tour of the carriage house proper?" Helena asked.

"Absolutely."

The tour took about thirty minutes and Randi seemed more enthralled with each room they visited, raving not only about the architecture but even the choice of colors, furnishings and artwork.

When they returned to the kitchen, Randi removed her laptop from her briefcase and sat it on the table. "Bev told me this place was a stunner, but this is much grander than I was expecting. From all indications, it's in excellent condition for a house almost a hundred years old."

"Mia did a terrific job of keeping it in good repair."

"That's important, but as we all know, you can never be certain what kind of structural problems you'll find when you start checking out these historic houses."

"A truth we've all learned from watching cable house remodeling shows," Helena admitted. Not that she was too worried about that. Mia's estate had left Helena more than enough assets to make any needed repairs to the property.

"Who was your grandmother's decorator?" Randi asked. "I have several clients who could use their advice."

"Mia was her own decorator, right down to the smallest details. Well, I did give her a few suggestions in the artwork department, but that's it."

"Then you both have excellent taste. I love the painting of the young couple running through the rain beneath beautiful French Quarter balconies."

"Thank you. That's actually my first prize-winning painting from a high school art contest."

"You painted that in high school?"

"Eleventh grade."

"Wow. Such talent. I know you said you were starting a new job at a Boston gallery, but I didn't know you'd be exhibiting your own work."

"Hopefully. If not, I'll just be selling others' creations and searching for new talent, but even that is exciting."

"I'm sure you'll be successful. You obviously had a very talented grandmother, as well. She perfectly captured the historic nature of the home without giving up comfort or convenience. That's a hard combo to come by."

"Then you don't think I'll have any trouble selling the property for a decent price?"

The awkward silence and the pained expression on Randi's face said more than words could have.

Helena cringed. "Is the real estate market that bad?"

"It's not actually the market that's the problem."

"Then what is it?"

"It's this particular property, or more to the point it's that Elizabeth Grayson was staying here with her great-aunt when she was murdered."

"People still need a place to live," Helena said, trying to make sense of Randi's concerns.

"I know, but the media hype isn't making this any

easier. Elizabeth was killed six months ago. The three previous victims of the alleged serial killer were murdered at six-month intervals almost to the day."

"We've passed that date," Helena said.

"But only by a few days. People who are familiar with the facts are on edge. It's as if they're all holding their collective breaths waiting for the killer to strike again."

Helena's frustration swelled. "Elizabeth was abducted off the streets. There's no evidence the killer ever set foot on this property."

"I'm not saying it's reasonable," Randi said, "but I have to level with you. Normally, this house would sell in days, might even set off a bidding war. In this climate of fear, all bets of a quick, lucrative sale are off."

"In other words, my property has a curse on it until the killer is arrested and there's nothing I can do about it?"

"Not necessarily. I just want you to be aware that you may be in for some lowball offers if you list the property immediately. If the killer doesn't strike again, this should blow over in a few months."

"Renters don't seem to be afraid of moving in," Helene said, clutching at the only positive thing she could see. "Bev said there's a waiting list of prospective renters."

Randi stared at the well-manicured nails on her left hand for a few seconds before lifting her gaze. "More bad news. The waiting list fell through, according to Bev. Your recently vacated apartment has not been rented. And Connor Harrington in 4-C gave a thirty-day notice yesterday."

Helena threw up her hands in exasperation. "Connor is single and muscular. I can't believe he's afraid of being the serial killer's next victim."

"I don't know what reason he gave, but I'm sure Bev will get back with you in a day or two on that," Randi explained.

It had taken weeks of soul-searching for Helena to make up her mind to sell her grandmother's beloved home and now that decision might have to be delayed.

One thing was for certain. She wasn't going to give Mia's beautiful home away at below what it was worth just because of the timing.

"I didn't mean to rain on your parade like this," Randi said. "We don't have to decide or sign anything today, but we can talk about how to proceed if you do decide to list with us."

"I suppose that's complicated, too."

"Not at all."

Helena felt a nagging pain starting at the back of her skull. "I'm a novice at selling real estate, so I have no idea where to start. I suppose I should alert the remaining tenants that I'm putting the house on the market."

"Let's don't jump the gun on that," Randi cautioned. "Unless the prospective owner plans to use the entire property for himself and his family, having the units already under lease will be an asset."

They spent the next hour talking about the advantages of working on upgrades and repairs before having the house appraised. Randi clearly knew her stuff and she patiently answered all of Helena's questions while basically alleviating none of her fears.

By the time they'd finished and gone over the selling contract, Helena felt as if she were drowning in details.

She stood and walked to the window that overlooked the courtyard. "I suppose I should run this new information by Pierre Benoit."

"Is that the man that Bev listed as one of your tenants?"

"Yes. He's a divorce attorney with an office in the downtown area. I hired a probate attorney to settle Mia's estate, but Pierre walked me though some of the legal hurdles."

She owed him a dinner for that since he'd refused to accept cash.

"I think I've given you enough to think about for one day," Randi said. "I don't want you to feel pressured, but if you're going to have two vacant units, it might be a good time to do any needed repairs or updates on those first."

"Good point. I hadn't expected so many complexities, but I'll sign the real estate agreement now," Helena said. "I've made the decision to sell. The hard part is already done."

"Are you sure?"

"I am." If she didn't change her mind in the time it took to pick up the pen and sign her name on several dotted lines.

Randi delayed her departure to take her through the agreement again over a second glass of tea. Signing was more stressful than Helena had expected. She did so love this house.

But the life she knew here was gone forever and she would love her life in Boston, too. She had to keep reminding herself of that.

They made small talk as they walked across the courtyard when they were finished. Randi paused near the fountain just long enough to catch a few drops from the cool spray in her outstretched right hand.

"Whoever gets this house and courtyard is going to be a very lucky buyer," Randi said as she was leaving.

Helena stood by the gate for a few minutes after she locked it behind Randi. A blue jay darted past her on its way to the nearest bird feeder. Graceful monarch butterflies fluttered among the blooms of a potted verbena.

She was mere steps away from French Quarter revelry, music and great food, yet this space had always been a peaceful haven. Perhaps her tenants no longer thought of it as safe.

If that bothered Connor Harrington, it must be a million times worse for Ella. Helena needed to find time to visit with her today.

She glanced up and then she saw *him*.

Hunter Bergeron—still, quiet, alone, standing on the edge of Ella's balcony. Old longings vibrated along her nerve endings as she met his gaze. Her insides melted.

It had been six years, but she would have recognized him anywhere. Tall and muscular. Same unruly brown hair. Same cocky way of standing, his thumbs hooked into his jeans pockets.

Her stomach knotted and she felt the burn of acid creeping up into her throat.

She'd tried to prepare herself for running into him while she was back in New Orleans. Just not in this courtyard. Not where it had all begun—and ended.

Traitorous recollections pounded her relentlessly.

Then, without even a wave of acknowledgment, he turned and disappeared back inside Ella's apartment. Helena wrapped her arms around her chest and bit her bottom lip so hard she tasted blood.

Had he even recognized her? Had she become no more than a distant memory of an infatuation gone bad? Or maybe he looked at it as a commitment he'd escaped just in time.

It didn't matter. There was nothing left of their relationship but regrets.

She should turn and go back inside before he left Ella's.

But she was still standing there as if in a paralyzing trance when Hunter stepped out of Ella's door and into the courtyard. Her insides quaked as he approached, but she managed to keep her head up and her breathing somewhat steady.

"Hello, Helena."

Hello. That was it, as if it hadn't been six years since the goodbye that almost destroyed her. Her resolve not to let him intimidate her strengthened.

"What are you doing here, Hunter?"

"Looking for you, for one thing. Police business. We need to talk."

Chapter Five

Helena stared him down like he was a coiled snake about to strike, waiting so long to respond he felt sweat pooling on his brow. She clearly had the temperature advantage in her white shorts and lacy, summery top.

He was wearing his usual plainclothes detective attire—jeans and a sports shirt with the neck unbuttoned and the sleeves rolled up to his elbows.

Nonetheless, he was starting to feel guilty as hell that he was ruining her homecoming by insisting she have anything to do with him.

He stepped closer. "This won't take long."

"Then start talking."

"I talk faster when I'm not sweltering."

"Does this have anything to do with Elizabeth Grayson's killer?"

He nodded. "Afraid so."

"In that case, we can talk inside."

He followed her into the carriage house. In minutes he'd settled into the same comfortable chair in Mia Cosworth's cozy sitting room as he had dozens of times before over the last few months. Surprisingly, he'd developed a close bond with Mia during this investigation though she'd clearly never forgiven him for running out on Helena. Made sense. He'd never forgiven himself.

Not only had Mia's death hit Hunter hard personally, it had blown a huge hole in his best lead toward catching the French Kiss Killer.

Helena sat across from him. She leaned back and crossed her long shapely legs.

She was as stunning as ever, but she'd changed in ways that hurt deep in his soul. He felt it as much as saw it, though her expression was stony, her eyes a cold fire that froze and burned at the same time.

"Why were you at Ella Grayson's this morning?" Helena asked.

Hunter crossed a foot over his knee. "I'd picked up some beignets at Café du Monde, and we shared them over coffee. She loves them heavy on powdered sugar—same as me—and she makes the best cup of coffee in town."

"I suppose I'm to believe delivering morning pastries to the elderly is a new service of the police department?"

Helena was clearly not going to make this easy.

"No official policy," he said, "but we're allowed to be decent."

Helena ran her fingers through her shoulder-length copper-colored hair, pushing it back from her bewitching face. "In that case, I apologize for doubting your motives."

"No problem. I'm not above playing good cop to get

information if I need to, but this time it was all about the donuts and coffee. And the fact that she's having a tough go of it."

He recognized the signs of depression. He'd grown up with them.

"I plan to see her as soon as you leave," Helena said. "We've kept in touch by phone since my grandmother died."

"She's mentioned that."

"I don't know why," Helena said, "but she seems to feel at least partly responsible for the tragedy, though there was nothing she could have done to save Elizabeth. I keep reminding her that Elizabeth was a random victim of a demented serial killer."

Hunter leaned in closer. This was likely as good a segue as he would get. Might as well take advantage of it.

"We're not sure about the random element."

Helena's brows arched. "Wasn't she abducted while on her way to meet friends?"

"Perhaps not. She'd told Ella that she was meeting friends, but her friends said the night out was planned for the following night. Elizabeth either confused the plans or lied to Ella."

"Do you think she deliberately met with the monster?"

"A definite possibility."

Helena clasped her hands in her lap. "Why would she do such a thing? How could he persuade her to go with him?"

"If we had the answer to those questions, we'd

have a lot better chance of stopping him before he strikes again."

"Then you think he will strike again?"

"I believe it's possible."

"I can't believe Elizabeth could be taken in by a murderous lunatic. She was so smart and sweet. She had plans and dreams. Mia said she talked about her future all the time."

Helena's voice shook and her eyes grew moist with tears as the new reality sank in.

Desire racked Hunter's body. Not sexual urges, but just a need to touch her, to wrap an arm around her shoulders, to hold her close.

But she made no move to indicate she wanted his comfort and he wasn't about to risk being tossed out at this point.

"Is there more I should know?" Helena asked.

"Yeah," he said. "None of it good."

"Tell me everything and start with the worst," she urged. "Don't spoon-feed me."

"You got it. Elizabeth's killer or a person claiming to be him was in touch with Mia by phone in the days preceding Mia's fall."

"The killer was contacting Mia? Why didn't I know about that? Why didn't someone tell me?" She straightened, her hands on her knees.

"She didn't want to upset you or disrupt your life when there was nothing you could do."

"I could have done something. I could have been here. She could have come and stayed with me. You should have told me." She leaned forward, and he saw fire in her eyes.

"She didn't want you to know. I had no authority to go against her will." Plus, she'd threatened Hunter eight ways to Sunday if he ignored her wishes and told Helena himself.

"How many times did he call her?"

"Three, over a three-week period."

"What did he talk about? Did he threaten her? Didn't you wiretap her phone?"

"How about one question at a time?" Hunter asked. "He admitted he'd killed Elizabeth." He wasn't about to go into the graphic way he described it to Mia in his first call. He hoped to hell Helena never had to hear those words and was relieved they hadn't been recorded, which would risk her hearing them.

"Did he threaten Mia?"

"No, but he was clearly upset that she was raising award money for his capture and assured her that he would kill again and that he wouldn't get caught."

"You must have traced the calls and found out who he was and where he was calling from. You can do that in minutes."

"You've been watching too many detective shows on TV. Real cops don't work miracles. We did wiretap her phone—after she reported the first call. When she answered the next two, the calls went straight to the precinct where they were monitored."

"Then why couldn't you track him?"

"The calls were from different numbers. The wire-tapped calls lasted less than a minute. By the time we could get to the location of origination, the caller and the phones were long gone."

"And Mia didn't recognize the caller's voice?"

"No. Three different voices were used—two appeared to be male, one was female."

"Then three different people were in on this?"

"Very unlikely. We believe a professional grade voice changer was used."

"Where is my grandmother's phone now?"

"In police custody. It hasn't rung since her death."

"Then he must have known her well enough to know when she died," Helena said.

"Maybe, but it made the local news. Your grandmother was pretty much a legend in this area what with all her charitable and historic preservation work."

Helena massaged her arms as if she were cold, the facts no doubt chilling her to the bone.

"I know this is not what you wanted to hear, Helena, but rest assured we'll apprehend this guy sooner or later. He'll make a mistake. Serial killers always do. And when he does, we'll get him."

"But how many other teens or young women will he kill before he makes that mistake?" Helena asked.

"I can't answer that." And that was what kept him up at night, what haunted his mind every hour of the day. That kind of evil had to come from devils residing deep in a person's psyche. Even the killer might not know when he'd succumb to the darkness and strike again.

"Had Mia not died the untimely way she did, she might have led us to Elizabeth's killer," Hunter said.

"Poor Mia. So much to deal with. How horrible to

spend the last few weeks of her life being intimidated by a madman who must have wanted her dead. Wanted it bad enough…"

"I know what you're thinking," Hunter interrupted. The haunted look in her eyes and the angst in her expression made it clear. "Mia wasn't murdered by the serial killer or anyone else, Helena. That possibility was thoroughly investigated. There was absolutely no evidence of foul play. Absolutely none."

"Thank God for that."

"If it was the killer's intent to intimidate her, he failed miserably," Hunter said. "Your grandmother considered herself part of the investigative team and she was good at it."

"She was always a fighter," Helena said.

Hunter planted both feet on the floor and leaned forward. "I have one very important request. I don't want you to discuss the phone calls with anyone. Not your best friend. Not Ella. Definitely not a reporter."

"Why?"

He hesitated, choosing his words carefully. He didn't want to frighten her, but he had to warn her. "There's an outside chance the killer may try to contact you now that you've returned to the carriage house."

"What makes you think he even knows I exist?"

"He mentioned you in the last call."

"What did he say about me?"

"Just that she had a beautiful granddaughter. He hoped you'd be visiting soon."

"And obviously, I did. For Mia's funeral, almost as if he knew Mia was going to die."

"There's no way he could have predicted the fatal fall. The important thing is that I need you to call me immediately if you get a suspicious phone call or if anything happens that makes you uneasy," Hunter warned. "Even if you think it's probably nothing— even if the person who makes you uneasy is someone you know."

"Right now, you're making me extremely uneasy."

"Don't be. I'll keep you safe. I promise, but you have to trust me and never hesitate to call me."

"What great timing I have, as if I'm part of the killer's welcoming committee."

"If I'd known you were coming this week, I would have suggested you put the trip off."

"It never dawned on me to check a serial killer calendar."

"Understandable." Hunter walked over, took her hand and pressed his card into her palm. Even that slight touch stirred the old vibes. He struggled to keep them under control.

"Put my cell phone number in your phone on speed dial. Call anytime, day or night. I'll always answer. Count on it."

She took the card, but quickly moved her hand away from his. "If that's all, you should go now. I'm sure you have more important work to do."

"Okay. Just remember, if you need me, I'm a phone call away and I can have a police officer here in seconds."

She walked him to the door and opened it.

"You always were a good cop, Hunter, even if you didn't know it. I'm glad you took it up again. You must have missed it."

"I missed a lot of things." Nothing as much as he'd missed her.

For a second, her gaze softened to velvet and he could almost swear he sensed a tinge of desire. But the moment passed, and she closed the door behind him.

She didn't want him around. He got that, but he had only two goals right now. To find the French Kiss Killer before he killed again and to keep Helena safe.

He planned to do both.

LEANING AGAINST THE closed door, Helena struggled to make sense of the disturbing emotions churning inside her. She felt like a cannonball had smashed into the house and ran over her, leaving her flattened and unable to react in any appropriate way.

Her first impulse had been to lash out at Hunter and blame him for Mia's having to deal repeatedly with a killer. He was the detective. He should have done more to find the killer or at least kept him from talking to Mia.

If nothing else, he should have at least called Helena and let her know about the phone calls.

Only her grandmother wasn't one to be ordered around by anyone—never had been. Instead of quivering in fear, she'd likely dived in just like Hunter said, knowing full well what she was doing and any risks she might be taking.

She was sixty-eight years old, but Mia had known no limits, accepted no boundaries. Helena would be lucky if she had half Mia's spunk at that same age.

Helena looked at the card Hunter had given her and realized she'd wadded it up in a clutched fist. She took it to the kitchen counter, laid it out flat and used her fingertips to iron out the wrinkles.

Call him if she needed him. She quaked at the thought.

Retrieving his last words from six years ago out of the depths of her memory, she used them like a suit of armor.

I'm sorrier than you'll ever know, but I can't go through with this.

And then he'd left her standing at the flower-bedecked altar like the fool she'd been. The fool she would never let herself be again.

Her phone rang. A quick surge of apprehension rocked through her.

"Hello."

"Helena, it's me, Ella. I hope I'm not disturbing you."

"Absolutely not. It's so good to hear from you. In fact, I was hoping to pay you a visit about eleven if that works for you."

"That would be great. We have so much to talk about now that you're moving back to New Orleans."

There was that bothersome misconception again. She'd clear that up when she saw Ella. The way things were going now, she couldn't get out of here fast enough. She slipped Hunter's card into her pocket.

ELLA MET HELENA at the door, greeting her with a bear hug that wouldn't quit. The clinging was an unnecessary but potent reminder of the angst Ella had been through over the last six months. When Ella finally pulled away, Helena took a good look at her and was shocked to see how much thinner and frail she'd become over the five weeks since Mia's death. The downward plunge in her health had begun months prior to that. Losing her best friend had only made it worse.

Before Elizabeth's murder, Ella had been so plump that her apron ties were barely long enough to make a bow in the back. Her cheeks had been fat and rosy, her hair smooth with a fair amount of brown.

Now, her flowered top practically fell off her shoulders and her blue, flour-stained apron was tied in a big bow. New wrinkles tugged at her mouth and puffy, dark flesh circled her eyes. Her hair was almost totally gray with frayed ends that barely reached the middle of her ears.

Selling the house and property might turn out to be a wash on this trip, but at least Helena could spend some quality time with Ella before she left for Boston.

Helena breathed in the odor of spices wafting from the kitchen. "What is that I smell?"

"Peach cobbler."

"My favorite," Helena said. "You remembered."

"How could I forget? Mia and I spent one whole day a few summers ago gathering peaches at a local pick-your-own orchard. Day was hotter than Lucifer's spa, but she refused to quit until she had enough of the juicy fruit to fill her freezer."

"I take it you did not handpick these peaches."

"Sure I did. Picked them right from the baskets at the French Market when they were at their peak. Then I sliced and froze them."

They both laughed, and it was amazing how much that softened the hard lines in Ella's face. She probably didn't laugh nearly enough.

"I didn't just make cobbler," Ella said. "I made some homemade shrimp salad. And I have fresh French baguettes to spread it on."

"You shouldn't have gone to all that trouble."

"Wasn't that much trouble. Besides I figured we'd have a lot more time and privacy for talking if we ate here. You know how noisy some of the lunch spots can be."

"Especially the ones worth going to where the seafood gumbo is hot and spicy and the po'boys drip all down your shirt."

"Well, when you put it that way, maybe we should have gone out," Ella said.

"Another day," Helena said. "Shrimp salad sandwiches, peach cobbler and being here with you in your comfy, air-conditioned apartment can't be beat."

Ella led the way to her second-floor kitchen.

All of the units were more or less what Helena considered upside down. Kitchen and dining areas and a spare room with floor to ceiling windows were on the second floor. Ella used her extra room for a guest room.

A large family area with a fireplace was on the first floor of every apartment as was a very spacious bedroom suite. All the apartments were entered through the courtyard. All had second-floor balconies and an ambiance that reeked of history and comfort.

Ella pointed to a bottle of white wine on the counter. "Would you mind opening the wine? I splurged on a bottle of Mia's favorite chardonnay and I've been saving it to celebrate your homecoming."

"Sounds great."

"I chilled it before you got here. Wineglasses are on the table."

They stuck to small talk until they'd settled at the dining nook that overlooked the myriad of greenery and blossoms trailing over the iron balcony.

They devoured the sandwiches and were halfway through bowls of warm cobbler topped with ice cream before the conversation took a nosedive.

"I saw you talking to Hunter Bergeron in the courtyard when he left here this morning," Ella said. "I'm glad to see the two of you are cordial again. Mia would be, too. I'm not sure she ever quite forgave him for backing out of the wedding, but she was convinced he was going to be the one to apprehend Elizabeth's killer."

First Alyssa and now Ella. It was as if Hunter had his own cheering squad. She had no intention of becoming one of his groupies.

"I hope he's successful in getting the killer off the streets," Helena said, "but I don't see the two of us becoming friends."

"Sorry. It was probably thoughtless of me to bring him up. I don't blame you for the bad feelings. It's just that you've both done a lot of growing up since then. I think you'd like him if you'd give him a chance."

"From what I hear, Hunter has plenty of friends."

"Mostly other detectives. He's asked about you several times," Ella added before letting the subject drop.

Helena was not about to get drawn into talk of what Hunter said or thought about her. Seeing him again had shaken loose a few old memories, but she would make certain things between them went no further.

They talked for at least an hour about the neighborhood and the other tenants and all the plans that were in the works for fall festivals.

Fortunately, they managed to avoid any further mention of Hunter and any talk about Elizabeth's murder, keeping things on the lighter edge of the spectrum.

Things had gone so well, Helena was stunned when she saw tears welling in Ella's eyes as she walked Helena down the stairs and to the door.

"I'm thrilled you're back, Helena. I promise not to be a burden, but you can't imagine how much your being close by means to me. I miss your grandmother so much. She held me together when I literally didn't think I could go on. She's the only one who understood how much I was hurting."

Ella's words felt like a jagged cord circling Helena's heart. "I know how close the two of you were, but you must have other friends you can talk to about your grief. It can't be good for you to keep it all bottled up inside you."

"I have lots of friends. They all try to help. Even Hunter comes by at least once a week. They say they understand, but they can't. It's not their pain. It's mine. Most of them had never even met Elizabeth."

"Your niece was beautiful in looks and spirit," Helena said. "I know how much you loved her."

"I still do, and I can't begin to heal as long as the monster who killed her is out there just waiting to take someone else's life."

"They'll find him and make him pay," Helena said, though she wasn't convinced of that herself. "Have you tried talking about your pain with Alyssa Orillon? Mia always said Alyssa had an uncanny talent for connecting with people."

"We talked a few times. I begged her to try to reach Elizabeth across the gulf of death. All she did was tell me to think about happy times Elizabeth and I had together. It didn't help. I'm just glad to have you back."

Helena couldn't leave it like this. A lie of omission even for a good reason was still a lie. "I hate disappointing you, Ella, more than you can know, but I'm not moving back to New Orleans."

"But Mia left all the property to you. It's yours free and clear."

"It is. But my life isn't in New Orleans. I've taken a new job in Boston that starts November 1. I'll be moving there permanently then or sooner if this property sells."

Ella stepped away. "But you loved this place. Mia had always counted on your moving here one day. You can't just put it in the hands of strangers."

It was useless to try to explain her own reasoning when at times she doubted the decision herself.

She took both of Ella's hands in hers. "Let's just take it a day at a time. Who knows? I may never find a buyer."

Ella sighed and shrugged. "You will. It just won't be a Cosworth."

Helena felt like she was deserting Ella as she walked away, but at least Ella would have Hunter around to pay her visits.

And for some crazy, inexplicable reason, that thought made Helena feel worse.

Chapter Six

Determined not to dwell all afternoon on a lunatic killer who had trolled her grandmother, Helena began the task of cleaning out Mia's closets. She'd been far too upset to tackle that when she'd been here for the funeral, although she had picked up numerous large plastic containers to simplify the process.

One pile for throwaway. One for items to keep. And one to be given away to local charities. She even had a fourth pile for items she though Ella might like.

Unfortunately, the task was much more difficult than she'd anticipated. There was basically nothing to throw away out of the linen closet. Mia had always been a neatnik, another of her admirable traits that hadn't been passed on to Helena. Everything was in excellent condition, many items unused.

Unfortunately, there was a fifth pile Helena hadn't counted on—the items Helena had no real use for but couldn't bear to part with.

The tablecloths Mia had used for the various holidays. The Easter one with a Peter Rabbit illustration had been Helena's favorite as a child. And then there were the lace table runners and doilies that they'd purchased the first time Mia had taken Helena to Scotland. And there were the cashmere throws Mia wrapped herself in to read or watch TV in front of the fireplace on cold winter nights.

That barely scratched the surface of the possessions Helena would love to keep, but as nostalgic as they might make her feel, they weren't Helena's style. She'd likely only be moving them from a closet in New Orleans to one in Boston to sit until they dry-rotted.

So, armed with the plastic containers and a will to keep only what was necessary while she lived in the carriage house, Helena began to put everything away and label accordingly.

It was nearly five o'clock when she finished. She stood and stretched, unkinking her tight muscles. When she walked into the kitchen to refill her water bottle, she noticed that the sun's hot rays were no longer beating against the windows.

A layer of dark clouds had moved in, threatening one of the late afternoon showers that were so common in this part of the South. No one complained much since the rain cooled things down a bit.

If she hurried, she might get in a walk and a chance to check on Alyssa before the storm hit. The more she thought about Alyssa's dizzy spell last night, the more it worried her.

Helena ran upstairs for her rain jacket, tossed her handbag over her shoulder and hurried out the door.

With her head lowered to block the breeze that had

kicked up, she practically ran into Pierre Benoit at the gate.

"Where are you off to in such a rush?" he asked. "Hot date?"

"No such luck. Only a walk around the neighborhood, hopefully before the thunderstorm breaks loose. If not, I'll duck into a shop and wait it out—or get wet. Water won't kill me."

"So, you're a walk in the rain kind of gal. Interesting."

"Warm rain. Not the icy downpours we get up North."

"Another good reason you should forget Boston and stay here."

Pierre was a fairly new tenant. He'd moved in shortly after Elizabeth's death and she'd only spent any time with him when she'd come home for Mia's funeral.

He'd been extremely thoughtful, offering to help in any way he could and then following up on that offer by phone when Helena had returned to her job.

He was far more handsome than she remembered. Dark eyes and a dimple in his chin. Expensively dressed in a black, pin-striped suit, every bit as professional looking as she'd expect of a successful attorney.

He smiled. "I saw your light on last night. I started to call and invite myself over for a nightcap, but I figured I'd best give you time to settle in."

"Thanks. I was exhausted but I'm fine today."

"Then how about dinner? There's a new French restaurant in the Garden District. Haven't tried it myself yet but the reviews all claim the food is *délicieux*."

"Now you're going to show off by going French on me."

"Obviously it will take more than that to impress you."

"I do owe you a dinner," she said.

"I ask a pretty woman to dinner, I pay."

"No way. Not after you gave me all that free professional advice. But I'm not hungry enough to do justice to an expensive restaurant or even a dive tonight. I overloaded on Ella's peach cobbler at lunch."

"Now I'm envious. What about tomorrow night?"

She could hardly say no since he'd been so helpful when she needed it. Besides, she might even enjoy his company. It would beat the chance of facing Hunter again with all the disturbing reactions he ignited.

"Seven?" he verified.

"Works for me."

She turned to leave, but not quickly enough.

"I suppose Hunter Bergeron has already stopped by to welcome you in his inimitable style," Pierre said.

"You don't make that sound like a compliment."

"Hardly. The detective's almost as enjoyable as a bonfire in August."

Hunter had his faults. Being likeable had never been one of them and from the way Mia and Ella talked about him that hadn't changed.

"What did he do to tick you off?" she asked.

"His general modus operandi."

"Which is?"

"Asking the same questions over and over in dozens

of different ways like he thinks if he harasses you long enough, you'll confess to something. Or maybe you'll suddenly remember seeing an abduction that had just slipped your mind before."

Hunter had always been persistent, except where she was concerned. It hadn't taken much to make him cut and run then.

"I'm surprised he hasn't driven off all your tenants by now," Pierre continued. "Only reason I'm still here is that I signed a year's lease."

"If Hunter is still asking questions, I'm sure he has a reason for it," Helena said, for some reason feeling she had to defend him. "He's a good detective."

Pierre shrugged. "If you say so."

"Mia trusted him," she said, by way of explanation. "Now I better get going if I'm going to beat the rain."

"Good luck with that."

"I'm prepared for the worst." She pulled her rain jacket tighter to make her point.

"Be careful," he called as she walked away.

"Be careful" had obviously become the new "See ya." A bit foreboding for her taste, as if disaster might be lurking around every corner. Or maybe it was just talking about Hunter that upset her.

She slid her hand into the front pocket of her crop pants as she reached the gate. Her fingertips brushed the edge of Hunter's business card. Call him anytime.

She wouldn't. She couldn't let herself fall under his spell again.

There was a metal trash receptacle near the curb.

She considered dropping Hunter's card in it. She'd punch in 911 before calling him to the rescue.

But the card remained in her pocket as she started on her walk.

ALTHOUGH NOT THE ideal day, it was pleasant enough for Helena to quickly relax among the familiar streets of the French Quarter. She walked to Jackson Square. The artists had taken their easels and left before the rain, but a young man in clown makeup risked the storm to make a few more dollars with his antics and balloon animals. The families standing around him seemed dismissive of the distant thunder, as well.

Helena turned and strolled to the city's famous Moon Walk, a promenade along the busy Mississippi River. A cruise ship was docked nearby and a steamboat paddled past it, the familiar music from its calliope making her feel even more at home.

As excited as she was about her new job in Boston, this area was the setting for her best memories. And her worst, thanks to Hunter. And here she was letting him take up space in her thoughts again.

Helena doubled back so that she'd pass Alyssa's. Following the printed instructions on the placard, she rang the bell. She was about to walk away when Alyssa finally came to the door.

"Did I come at a bad time?" Helena asked.

"I'm with a customer. I won't be but five minutes longer. Can you wait?"

"Sure, or I can come back tomorrow. I just wanted

to make sure you're not having any more of those dizzy spells."

"There's a story there," Alyssa said, "but I think I have it all figured out."

"That sounds a bit mysterious." The good news was Alyssa's face was no longer ashen and her smile much more natural.

Her long, colorful skirt made whispery sounds, background for her jangling bracelets and dangling earrings as she ushered Helena into the waiting room.

"There's water, wine, coffee or soft drinks in the fridge. Help yourself."

The odor of fresh brewed coffee lured Helena to the small room Alyssa used as a convenient living area near her workspace. By the time she'd poured herself a cup and taken a few sips, Alyssa was seeing her customer to the door.

She turned her sign to Closed.

"Don't lose paying customers on my account," Helena insisted.

"Believe me, I need a rest after Annabelle. She's in here every week with a new problem she wants me to solve. This time she thinks her husband is having an affair because he doesn't talk to her at bedtime. My bet is he can't get a word in edgewise."

"Well, you should know. You're the psychic."

"I'm not, but I'm starting to feel like one and that's downright scary."

"Tell me more."

Alyssa took the other chair. "I think it's all related to

the French Kiss Killer, though I hate that something as sexy as a French kiss is tied to something so depraved."

"How did he get that nickname?"

"No one seems to know, or if they do they're not admitting it. At any rate, I have the feeling that he is just about ready to strike again. Not psychic, more like how my arthritis lets me know the weather is changing."

"A lot of people seem to have that same intuition these days."

Helena didn't believe in psychics, but she didn't necessarily not believe in them, either. Some people might have a sixth sense, sort of the way she saw visions in her head before she painted them.

"There's more," Alyssa said. "I'm starting to feel like I'm caught up in a horror movie."

"How's that?"

"Two very attractive young women were in here earlier and one of them reminded me of Elizabeth. Not just her looks, though I swear they could pass as twins—both as beautiful as supermodels. It was also her personality. You know, lively and charismatic."

"Some people think everyone has a double," Helena said, doubting they were exactly alike. "I can see how seeing Elizabeth's double might shake you up, but Elizabeth was an only child, so no mysterious twin sister."

"But what if the serial killer is still in this area? If Elizabeth was his type, then this lady must be, too."

"You have a point there. Do you have the young woman's name or know how to get in touch with her?"

"All I know is that her friend called her Lacy and they're staying at the new boutique hotel on Decatur."

"The Aquarelle?"

"That's it. Not a name that sticks to the tip of your tongue."

"I've never been in that hotel," Helena admitted. "You really think this young tourist could be in danger, don't you?"

"It's this niggling fear that won't go away."

"You should call Hunter. If nothing else, you'll feel better if you share your concerns with him."

"He'll think I'm crazy."

"At least you'll know you did what you could. Now I should get out of here before we get a downpour and I have to swim back to the carriage house."

"Okay. Thanks for stopping by, and I think I will give Hunter a call."

"It can't hurt," Helena agreed. She stood to leave. "One other thing," Helena said as she reached the door. "If seeing someone who reminded you of Elizabeth set off your concerns today, what had you so rattled last night? Was that another specific intuitive moment or just general serial killer-induced fear?"

Alyssa hesitated. "Last night I..." She shook her head. "I don't know. It could have been that I was just excited about seeing you."

That made no sense, but Helena let it go. Alyssa seemed to have enough to deal with for now.

HELENA MADE A sudden detour that would take her right past the Aquarelle Hotel. Not that she expected to run into the two tourists Alyssa had described, but it was possible. Her curiosity was definitely piqued.

The serial killer scenario was playing weird tricks on her mind as well, especially knowing that he'd actually talked to Mia by phone.

A streak of lightning split the dark clouds followed by a loud clap of thunder. She instantly regretted making the turn onto Decatur. The first drops of rain pelted her when she was a few feet from the hotel's canopied door.

Instead of raising her umbrella, she made a run for it, making it to cover just in time not to get soaked.

The reception area was empty except for a couple who appeared to be checking in and a bellboy manhandling a cart overflowing with luggage.

As expected, there was no sign of the young woman who'd thrown Alyssa into a tumultuous tizzy.

A quick stop at the ladies' room to finger brush her slightly damp hair away from her face and then Helena followed the carpeted walkway to the bar area.

It was not only busy but ringing with loud voices and laughter as you'd expect from revelers visiting the French Quarter on a stormy late afternoon.

If anyone here was panicking over a serial killer on the loose, they were doing a good job of hiding it. Helena scanned the room and found the perfect spot for people-watching, a table near the end of the bar with a view of everyone who came or went.

Truth be told, she felt a bit like a spy, searching for the type of young woman the killer might be looking for. That was also a little sick. She needed a martini and a jolt of reality. She was neither a spy nor a detective and wouldn't know a clue if it sat down beside her.

Within minutes she was sipping a lemon drop martini from a sugar-frosted glass. Rain continued to splatter the windows. An attractive, middle-aged woman trilled the keyboard at a grand piano near the front of the bar.

Within minutes the music paired with alcohol soothed Helena's troubled mind. She sipped slowly.

The lights lowered after a half hour or so. More customers wandered in and happy hour began to morph into the dinner hour. The waitress stopped by to see if Helena wanted another drink before the happy hour prices disappeared.

The offer was tempting, but she resisted. She wanted her mind clear if she decided to check out more of Mia's highlighted material or handwritten notations in her research sources.

She jerked to attention when a tall man stopped at her elbow.

"Hello, Helena."

It took her a second to recognize her soon-to-be moving tenant.

"Hi, Connor. I was hoping to run into you. I just didn't expect it to be so soon."

"I saw a light on in the carriage house last night and figured you were home," he said. "We've all been wondering when you'd move back and take over. Are you having dinner with us tonight?"

"With *us*?"

"Yes, here at the hotel. I'm the food and beverage manager at the Aquarelle Hotel now."

"I didn't know. You must be doing a lot of things

right. The place is hopping, and my lemon drop martini was superb."

"Nice to hear. Would you like another drink?"

"Thanks, but I'll pass on that this time. How is the position working out for you?"

"I'm loving the job so far. The work is challenging but rewarding and the pay is much better than I was making managing that bar on Bourbon Street."

"Moving on up. Is that why you're giving up your lease on your apartment?"

"You heard? Sorry about that. I'd have told you in person if I'd known you were coming back here so soon. I hate to leave. Three years, that's the longest time I've ever lived anywhere since I left home to go to LSU."

"I hate to see you go. Why are you leaving?"

"I've got a new girlfriend."

"Sounds serious."

Connor nodded. "I think this may be the one, and I figure it's time I settle down with one woman. I'll be thirty-two next week."

"When's the wedding?"

He shoved his hands into his front trouser pockets and grinned. "Not quite that serious yet. We've decided to cohabit for a few months first. You know, make sure our clothes can stand tossing around in the wash together."

"So, you'll be moving in with her?"

"No way. Her bathroom is barely big enough for two toothbrushes and I'd never fit my clothes into her one tiny closet."

"Then why move?" Helena asked. "The apartment you're in has quite a bit of storage and a roomy bathroom if I remember correctly."

"Yeah. The size is great, but my lease specifies one occupant."

"That's probably because you were single when you signed it. We could update that."

He pulled out a chair. "Mind if I join you for a few minutes?"

"Of course not."

"There is another issue," he said, keeping his voice low, obviously not wanting to be overheard by his hotel guests. "Hannah's all hung up with this serial killer hype. Says she'd be afraid to ever stay by herself in my apartment."

"Did you explain that there's no evidence that Elizabeth's killer was ever on the carriage house property?"

"A dozen times. The only way my staying in the apartment is going to work is if the French Kiss Killer gets arrested—which I keep thinking is bound to happen soon. Detective Bergeron is a cop on a mission. No doubt about it."

And now they'd circled back to Hunter. Was every discussion in this town destined to do that?

"Do you see a lot of Hunter Bergeron?" she asked.

"Not lately, but I ran into him fairly often when your grandmother was alive. She raised a lot of money to help the police catch the killer. So far it hasn't helped."

"Did you ever feel like Hunter was interrogating you more than necessary?"

"No way. Where did you get that idea? He asked

some questions. That's his job. I only wish I'd had some answers for him. Nice teenager like Elizabeth. She deserves justice."

"How well did you know Elizabeth?"

"I'd only seen her to say hello when she was visiting Ella until her last trip down here. Then we sat around the fountain a couple of nights and talked about her graduating high school and heading off to college."

Connor pushed back in his chair. "I wish we'd talked more. Then I might have been able to tell Hunter something useful to the investigation."

"We all wish that."

"I better get back to work now." Connor stood, adjusted his tie and smoothed his well-fitting sport coat. "Welcome back to New Orleans," he said. "Your drink's on the house. I'll let your waiter know."

"Thanks."

"Yeah. Sorry about moving. I really like living there. Not much chance we'll find another courtyard as beautiful as yours."

The rain had slowed to a gentle mist when she left the hotel and started home. There was still no sign of Lacy and her friend.

HELENA SLOWED AS she approached home. Her heart jumped to her throat when she spotted Hunter leaning against the gate, his right foot propped against the metal scrolls behind him, his thick hair mussed as usual. No one should look that good.

"Are you looking for me," she asked, "or is this more of your good-cop routine?"

"A little of both. We need to talk."

"We just did that a few hours ago."

"Something new has come up since then."

"Something that has to do with Alyssa Orillon?"

"Ahh. Another psychic in our midst."

Hardly. If she were, she would have seen her breakup with Hunter coming in time to pull out with some of her dignity intact. When she ignored the question, he punched in the code, pushed the gate open and stepped back to let her enter first.

"Who gave you the code?" she asked as he followed her into the courtyard."

"Your grandmother. She considered me one of the good guys. This would probably work easier if you did, too."

"I knew you better than she did."

"Touché. Now that the rain's stopped, how about we walk over to Maspero's and grab a sandwich and coffee? I could use some grub. Lunch lost out to a new lead and a request for a warrant."

"Anything to do with the serial killer?" she asked.

"A drug deal gone bad. A machete attack among the crypts in an Algiers cemetery. On second thought, omit that last sentence. Not an appetizing addition to a dinner invitation."

Not appetizing at all, but Maspero's was. Thinking of their infamous muffulettas made her mouth water. Unfortunately, having dinner with Hunter, even in a restaurant as casual and noisy as Café Maspero, would be playing with fire.

"Thanks, but no thanks, on the dinner invitation. Let's keep this strictly business."

"It was always going to be business, but people have to eat."

"I'd rather get this over with as quickly as possible," she said. "We can talk inside."

"Making me the enemy is not going to keep you safe or help me stop a killer."

She nodded, knowing she was more afraid of her reactions than his. She could pretend that her heart had healed completely, but her body wasn't convinced.

They went inside, but this time settled at the small table in the kitchen. "I can offer you coffee."

"Love some."

She could have probably rustled up something more filling, but the more personal this became, the more risk to her emotions.

Hunter took two cups from the cupboard and the carton of half-and-half from the fridge while she started a pot of coffee. He'd obviously spent enough time with Mia that he felt right at home.

"How well do you know Alyssa Orillon?" he asked.

"We're not close, but I've known her since I was a kid. She and Mia were friends, so I guess I kind of inherited her as a friend."

"Do you think she's credible?"

"As a psychic?"

"In general."

"She's honest about her mystic abilities—or lack thereof—unless you go by the sign on her door. Advertisements usually contain a bit of hyperbole. So, yeah, I don't see why she'd lie about her intuitions or about her customers."

"Specifically, one named Lacy," he verified.

"Right."

"Then we're on the same page."

Hunter waited until Helena served the coffee before saying more. "I've never given any credibility to the sixth sense sort of predictions. I like solid facts and concrete evidence.

"On the other hand, I frequently rely on hunches and some of the older guys on the force swear there were times Alyssa's grandmother provided them with information that defied reason."

"Then you think Alyssa's fears are legitimate."

Hunter sipped his coffee. "Legitimate enough that we should check them out. All four of his victims fit the same general description, which means Lacy fits it, too."

"Is that typical with serial killers?"

"There are no hard-and-fast rules, but sometimes appearance seems to be part of the motivation for the next crime. And if Lacy looks that much like Elizabeth, she could be a trigger. That is assuming the killer is anywhere near the French Quarter.

"In a space the size of New Orleans and the surrounding area, the chances they'd cross paths are slim to none."

Helena ran her finger over the top of her cup while her mind played with possibilities. "What will you tell Lacy that won't frighten her and her friend to death?"

"I'll talk it over with the rest of the task force. The

best option may be having an undercover female detective befriend them and warn them about hooking up with strangers even if they seem perfectly safe. She can also chat with them enough to find out if they've already been hit on. If so, we'll follow up on that."

"I can't imagine Lacy and her friend would just instantly bond with an undercover cop."

"That's where the competence of our undercover officers pays off."

"Wouldn't it be something if Alyssa earned the reward money Mia helped collect?"

"We're talking long shot here," Hunter reminded her. "The killer's been quiet for over six months. He could have moved out of this area completely. He may have been killed in a car crash or died of some cruel disease, though that's likely too much to ask for."

Helena was relieved to hear Hunter hadn't just brushed off the info from Alyssa, but she didn't see how she fit into this.

"Why rush over here to talk to me before even stopping to grab a bite or get down to the business of checking out Lacy?"

Hunter finished his coffee before answering, visibly avoiding what should be a simple response as to why he was here. Finally, he stretched one hand across the table as if he were reaching for her hand.

Instinctively, she pulled her hand away and placed it in her lap. One touch and the wall of heartache and regret separating them might disintegrate.

Hunter pulled back his hand and propped his elbows

on the table. "Lacy and her friend were not the only women who caused Alyssa to see frightening images."

"There were others? Who? When?"

"Only one. You. Last night."

"Alyssa didn't mention disturbing visions to me. She was dizzy but said it was nothing to worry about."

"She didn't want to frighten you," Hunter explained.

"And you do?"

"No. I want to keep you safe."

This made no sense. Alyssa had to be mistaken. "What kind of vision did she see?"

"She saw you, covered in blood, being chased by a man with a knife."

"Who was the man?"

"His face was too blurry to tell."

This was growing more bizarre by the second. "Alyssa must be hallucinating. She's so scared by all this talk of the French Kiss Killer, she's seeing danger everywhere—just like everyone else in this town."

"Probably, but I thought you should know, especially since you went looking for trouble today instead of avoiding it."

"I don't know what you mean."

"You headed straight for the Aquarelle Hotel when you left Alyssa's this afternoon."

"How do you know that? Are you having me followed?"

"Not yet. I dropped by the hotel after talking to Alyssa. You were in the bar talking to Connor Harrington, about what I don't know. But we both know you were there because of what Alyssa told you."

"There's no law against having a drink in a hotel lounge," she quipped.

"No, but there is a law against interfering in an investigation. It's also dangerous."

He finished off his coffee and pushed his cup away from him. "I need to see your phone."

This was going too far. Helena stood and backed away from the table. "I wasn't interfering with anything and I don't need your protection. I'm not afraid."

"Of course you're not. You're Mia Cosworth's granddaughter. Now hand me your phone and I'll program my number into it and put it on speed dial."

She couldn't argue anything he said, so she laid her phone down on the table in front of him. "I don't expect the killer to contact me."

"Good. Neither do I."

"And I'm not planning to go looking for trouble."

"Also good because I'd hate to put you under house arrest."

"On what grounds?"

"I'll think of something."

He was surely bluffing. When he finished with the phone, she walked him to the door.

Instead of leaving, he held the door open and looked down at her, his gaze burning into hers. He leaned closer until his lips were only inches away from her mouth.

Old urges erupted inside her, a hunger that she'd thought was lost forever.

"Play this smart. Stay safe, Helena," he murmured. And then he turned and was gone.

UNWILLING TO SUCCUMB to unbidden memories starring Hunter Bergeron, Helena spent the next two hours buried in one of Mia's nonfictional horror tales. The book on the twisted and horrifying backgrounds of famous criminals made her blood run icy; she upped the temperature control to eighty and still shivered beneath a light blanket.

Mia had made dozens of notations in the book, but none that made a lot of sense to Helena. The only obvious deduction from them was that Mia was trying to figure out how to use the book's contents to help her understand the man who had killed Elizabeth—a madman who in the last few weeks of her life insinuated himself into more than her mind. He'd literally tormented her with his phone calls.

When Helena had all she could stomach for one night, she kicked off the blanket and walked onto her balcony. There were no crowds this late on a Wednesday night, but she could hear music coming from somewhere and laughter and loud talk coming from a group of young adults hanging out on a balcony down the block.

Normal people going on with their lives. She had to get back to that. She had faith that eventually law enforcement would win. The infamous French Kiss Killer would be apprehended and either be killed or face a lifetime in prison.

But when and how many more innocent young women would he kill first? That was the question Hunter personally faced every day. Yet, even with that no doubt haunting his every breath, he'd found time to see her twice today.

Was that all typical police business or perhaps from an allegiance he felt toward Mia? Or was he looking for more from her?

Did he still have romantic feelings for her? Did he think they had a chance to recapture the love they'd once shared?

If so, he was wrong. It had been six years. Her physical and emotional reactions were betraying her. Hunter had destroyed the love and trust she'd felt for him on her wedding day.

The wedding that had never happened.

She walked back inside, showered, brushed her teeth and put on a pair of cotton pj's. Once she'd climbed into bed, she switched off her reading lamp and snuggled beneath the covers.

Hopefully she'd sleep without dreams. In the present situation they'd inevitably become nightmares.

In the foggy sphere between wakefulness and sleep, she heard her phone ring.

Chapter Seven

Helena jerked to an upright position, her heart pounding. Late-night phone calls were always alarming, but this was far worse than the usual trace of dread.

This was her cell phone, not Mia's home phone. That had been disconnected a few days after the funeral. There was no reason to think this could be Elizabeth's killer, but still she hesitated to answer the call.

She checked the ID. There was none. She checked the time. It was a few minutes before two a.m.

Reluctantly, she took a deep breath and pressed the answer button. "Hello."

There was no response, but she could hear heavy breathing through the connection.

"Hello," she said again.

Still no response.

Resolve attacked her fear. "You have ten seconds to answer before I hang up."

"Je ne le ferais pas si j'étais toi."

French. The French Kiss Killer. It had to be him, except that he sounded like a young, mischievous boy. Hunter had warned her the caller used a machine to create a robotic voice disguised like either gender. She hadn't expected it to sound like a kid voice.

She knew some French, enough that she knew he was warning her not to hang up.

"What do you want?"

"To welcome you home. *Bienvenue à la maison.*"

"Did you kill Elizabeth Grayson?"

"You are curious like your grandmother and to the point. I like that. Yes, Elizabeth's death was one of my great achievements."

"How could you commit such a sick crime? How could you kill a woman with her whole life in front of her?"

"Lots of people die before their time."

"She didn't just die. She was murdered—by you. The police are closing in on you. You're going to rot in jail."

He laughed. The disguise did not hide his madness. "I'm much too smart for the police. They are a joke."

"What do you want from me?"

"I'm not sure yet, but torture is more satisfying when you share it. Give Hunter my regards. Good night and sweet dreams."

The connection went dead, yet the voice felt as if it were vibrating through every vein in her body.

Helena no longer had a choice. She punched in Hunter's number.

HUNTER REACHED OUT the front car window to retrieve his food with one hand and for his ringing phone with the other. Damn these full moons that seemed to bring out all the crazies. It was two a.m. He should have been off duty hours ago. He needed food and sleep before he collapsed.

He thanked the worker and pulled away from the serving window before checking his caller ID. Helena. His heart slammed into his chest. Something big had to have happened for her to call him.

"What's wrong?" he asked in lieu of a greeting.

"I think the French Kiss Killer just called."

Adrenaline struck like a tidal wave. "What did he say?"

"That he called to welcome me home. Only he did it with a young boy's voice. That made it all the more chilling."

"No doubt. What else did he say?"

She repeated every word of their conversation, if not verbatim, then close, she assured him.

"Okay. I'm five minutes away, tops."

"You don't need to rush over here. Seriously, I'm not panicking now, though I may have been on the verge at first. I just thought you should know."

"You think? We're talking a killer here."

"I'm not suggesting he's not dangerous, but he was on the phone, not on the premises. The gate is locked. The dead bolts to the house are locked. Besides, from what you said earlier, his method is only to intimidate with phone calls."

His method up to this point. Who knew when that might change? They were dealing with a murderous madman.

"Keep the doors locked until I arrive. I have the

courtyard code and an emergency key to the house, both given to me by your grandmother. So don't take me for the lunatic and shoot me when I reach the door."

"I don't have a gun."

"We'll remedy that."

"I don't know how to shoot."

"We'll remedy that, too."

He attached the portable flashing lights to the roof of his unmarked sedan and revved up the sirens as he maneuvered the narrow streets of the French Quarter.

He needed this tie to the killer. Needed any link that might lead to a decent clue and his capture. But why the hell did it have to come via Helena?

Six years of regret bucked inside him like a wild bull. He blocked it the way he had in Afghanistan when his buddies' lives were at stake.

When push came to shove, a real man did what he had to do.

ONCE THE CALL to Hunter had been made, the sense of terror began to ease. The killer had called Mia for weeks with no physical confrontation.

It might not even be the real killer. For all she knew it was just some crazy person making crank calls. A way to boost his own self-importance with little risk— until he got caught. Maybe he only called when he was on a drug high.

There was no time to dress or put on makeup before Hunter arrived, and even if there were, Helena refused to go to any trouble to look attractive for him. She pulled on her short robe and shoved her feet into her slippers. A quick brush of her disheveled hair and she headed down the stairs and took up guard position at the door.

Concentrating on calming her nerves, she took deep breaths, exhaling slowly. He had the code to the gate. He wouldn't need to be buzzed into the courtyard or let into the house for that matter.

At this moment that was more comforting than disconcerting. The doorbell rang minutes before she expected him to arrive. She put her eye to the peephole to verify it was him before she opened the door.

He burst inside carrying a large paper bag that reeked of peppers and onions.

"You couldn't have stopped for food and gotten here this quickly without a jet engine," she said.

"I had the burgers and fries, just not time to eat them. Sorry for bringing it in with me, but I'm famished. Still getting by on the coffee you gave me earlier."

"You haven't been to bed yet?"

"No, but I was about to head that way when I got your call."

"Then we'll talk in the kitchen while you indulge in your unhealthy feast."

He followed her, dropping his bag to the table. "Are you okay?"

"Yes. I told you that on the phone. You didn't have to rush over here tonight. This could have waited until daylight."

His brows arched. "Now you're going to tell me how to do my job?"

"Of course not, but if my grandmother could handle talking on the phone with the monster without having hysterics, I'm sure I can, too."

"Point made."

He dropped into a kitchen chair. She took the one opposite his.

Here they were, sitting in the cozy kitchen again. He was here as a police officer, but they were connecting on a far more personal level and that's where the real risk came in.

They'd bonded the first time they'd met when she was only nineteen, gone straight from strangers to lovers in less than a week, skipping over all the steps in between. She had no idea where this step would have fallen in their failed relationship, but she knew where it couldn't go.

"Tell me everything," he said.

"I did. Even with the heavy breathing at the beginning, the call probably lasted less than a minute. How many times did you say he called Mia?"

"Three times over a three-week period. All extremely brief. By the end, she was convinced he was reaching out for help, trying to keep himself from killing again."

"What do you believe?"

"That there's a good chance he was just playing her."

He took a huge bite of his hamburger, then wiped his mouth on a paper napkin from his bag.

"Let me get you a plate," Helena offered.

"This is fine. Eating at a table instead of on the run

is luxury enough for me. Some milk would be good if you have it, though."

She poured him a glass of milk and set it in front of him. "Did the killer speak French to Mia, too? Is that how you came up with the name of French Kiss Killer?" she asked.

"Actually, it was because one of the crime scenes was on swampland previously owned by a well-known Cajun criminal. No one outside the task force knows about the phone calls."

"Are you sure the caller is the killer and not some crazy fake trying to get attention?"

"I'm ninety-nine percent sure he's the killer."

"Why?"

"He said a couple of things to Mia that only the killer would know."

"What kind of things?"

"Details about the murder itself that were never released to the public."

"So information only cops would have."

"Only a very limited number of cops and a couple of FBI agents working as advisers on the task force."

"Then maybe he was reaching out for help," Helena said. "And now that Mia's dead, he came to me, perhaps hoping I'd take over where she left off."

"He's a brutal serial killer who's already taken four innocent lives," Hunter stressed yet again. "I'm not saying this to frighten you. Well, maybe I am, but just enough to make sure you don't fancy yourself his therapist and do something foolish."

"I'm an artist, not a therapist. What do we do next?"

"For starters, someone will be over here probably around nine o'clock in the morning to put special software on your cell phone that will let us monitor and hopefully trace the origin of his calls."

"*All* my calls will be monitored by the police? That severely limits my privacy."

"All calls that come to your present cell phone. Be aware of that when you answer. The department will provide you with a phone to use for personal calls. You are to give that number only to people you fully trust. Like me."

"I can still use the internet, can't I?"

"Yes, but no social sites. Just to be safe, you should change your email address and all your passwords."

"You think Elizabeth's killer is also a hacker?"

"Isn't everybody?"

"Now you're being facetious."

"Sorry. I tend toward sarcasm after a day like this." He took another bite of his burger, catching a sliced jalapeño with his tongue as it slid from the bun.

"Do I still answer the suspect's calls?" she asked.

"Right. Just like you did tonight. We can assume that he has your private cell phone number and already knows you're back and living in Mia's carriage house."

She'd already figured out that much on her own.

Hunter finished off the first burger and unwrapped a second. "Are you sure you don't want half of this?"

"No, but thanks. Is there anything else I should know?"

He swallowed and wiped his mouth on one of the paper napkins from the food bag.

"A few rules," he said. "The most important is that I need to know where you are every second of the day and who you're with."

"Why? I know the risks. I'm not going to walk into a dangerous situation."

"Standard protocol and the fact that the man making the calls might also be stalking you."

"Did he stalk Mia?"

"No, but we can't take any chances with this man. You may be tailed when you leave the house, but you'll never see the undercover cop. On the other hand, if you notice someone who appears to be following you or if you seem to be running into the same person at different spots, call me at once."

It finally hit her. "This is about more than phone calls. Do you think he's targeting me as his next victim?"

"I'm just covering all the bases."

"Elizabeth was eighteen. I'm twenty-five. She was a blonde. My hair's auburn. I can't possibly fit his victim profile."

"Like I said, we're just covering all the bases. There is another option," Hunter said. "You should consider leaving the city and going back to where you've been living."

"That would get me out of your hair, but it wouldn't guarantee the monster wouldn't track me down. Besides, if I leave, you lose your best chance of contact with the killer. You have to admit that's true."

"You're not in law enforcement. Catching killers

is not your responsibility." He pushed his carton of French fries toward her.

She reached for one and popped it in her mouth. Next to chocolate, grease and salt had to be the best food therapy there was.

She did have options. Her new job didn't start until November 1. Thanks to the estate settlement, she had enough cash to travel. Spend a month in Italy or Greece, jet set around Europe and hope the police apprehended the killer before he struck again.

Or she could stay here and be neck deep in an investigation she had no control over—unless she forced a few issues.

This time she dipped her fry into ketchup before eating it. "I'm staying here," she said. "I'll follow your orders but first I want to hear all of the phone conversations between Mia and the killer that you have recorded."

"I'm not at liberty to share those with you."

"Then I'm not playing by your rules. I'll deal with the killer my way. Who knows? I may be the one who'll save him and the next victim."

She was bluffing. He probably guessed that since she wasn't nuts, but they both knew he could share those calls with her if it helped his case.

He stuffed the last bite of burger in his mouth, wadded his trash and shoved it into the bag. He chewed and swallowed and then stared at her for a few long minutes before agreeing to her terms.

"You drive a hard bargain, one that you may be

sorry for. But I'll arrange for you to hear the recordings, probably later today, after we both get some sleep."

That was much easier than she'd imagined.

He took his vibrating phone from his pocket. "I have to take this call."

"Sure. You're welcome to use the sitting room if you need privacy."

"Thanks."

She straightened the kitchen and disposed of the trash. He was still on the phone, so she went upstairs to make notes on her computer about all the things they'd discussed.

It was a good half hour before she came back downstairs. He had a key. He'd likely let himself out the door and locked it behind him.

Still, she checked the sitting room. He was on the sofa, his head half on a throw pillow, his shoes still on his feet, hanging off the end of the plaid couch.

He was fast asleep.

She trembled, suddenly rocked by a longing that left her weak and dizzy. She ached to lie down beside him and spoon her body with his.

And if he pulled her closer... If he burrowed his face in her hair... If she felt his warm breath on her neck...

The past would come back and devour her.

She pulled one of Mia's crocheted afghans from the large basket at the foot of the sofa and laid it across him.

She made it back to her own bed, but it was dawn before she fell asleep.

IT WAS DAYLIGHT when Helena opened her eyes again. Seven o'clock. She stretched, her left foot poking out from between the cool sheets. The AC was already whirring softly. It would probably be another scorcher today.

It was only Thursday, Helena's third day back in New Orleans. Already, Alyssa Orillon had envisioned Helena covered in blood and being chased by a mystery man yielding a knife. She'd learned her grandmother had a secret, dangerous life before her death. A man known as the French Kiss Killer had called Helena for no apparent reason.

And Hunter Bergeron had slept in her house for part of the night.

The reality of all of that sank in slowly as a surge of perplexing emotions rode the ragged endings of her nerves.

She punched her pillow a couple of times as if that could release her frustration before bracing herself to go downstairs and see if Hunter was still here. More likely, he'd dozed an hour or two and then gotten up and let himself out.

Her mouth tasted gritty. She brushed her teeth, washed her face and hit her hair with a few brushstrokes before piling it on top her head and fastening it down with a pair of large clips.

Even with all that was going on in her life, she hesitated on the stair's landing. Her beautiful grandmother who'd given so much of her time to making life brighter for others had spent the last days of her life in a mental war with a murderous monster.

That was reason enough for Helena to stay here and take over where Mia had been forced to leave off.

The house was silent when Helena reached the bottom of the stairs. No rhythmic breathing. No sounds of movement. Hunter was gone. She knew it from the sense of emptiness that stuck in her throat even before she reached the sitting room.

The afghan she'd thrown over him last night was neatly folded and resting on the arm of the sofa. The indentation of Hunter's head was still visible in the throw pillow.

She picked up the pillow to fluff it. Instead she put it to her face. It smelled of musk and soap and burgers. It smelled of Hunter and a new rush of old memories came crashing down on her.

She fought the onslaught by hurrying out of the room before she dropped to the couch and pushed against the cushions that had held his body a few hours ago.

Think of the past, she reminded herself. *The two of you made love like there was no tomorrow and then he walked away with no explanation.*

He'd had problems. She'd known that. He was under investigation for a mistake he'd made while doing his job. A mistake that had cost a life.

But instead of seeing it through, he'd just walked away. Whatever he'd needed to get past his problem, it hadn't been her. No reason to think he was a different man today. No reason to believe he wouldn't break her heart again if she gave him half a chance.

HUNTER HAD OVERSTEPPED all the boundaries last night. He should never have gone to sleep at Helena's place, but a full stomach and sheer exhaustion had called the shots. He'd closed his eyes for a second. When he'd opened them, it was five in the morning.

Fortunately he'd managed to let himself out of the carriage house without waking her.

Mess up this investigation and it could cost lives. Lose Helena's trust and she might not let him stick around to protect her. She was a lot like her grandmother—both too independent to take orders they didn't respect.

He paced her kitchen now while his partner, Cory Barker, showed her how the new phone app worked. She'd been distant with Hunter when he'd arrived first, but she appeared to be bonding with Barker just great.

"That's it," Barker said. "It's simple on your part, Ms. Cosworth. Answer the phone when it rings and try to keep our alligator goon talking as long as you can. Time is the major factor here if we're going to find and apprehend him before he dumps or destroys the phone and disappears."

"What should I say to keep him talking?" Helena asked.

"We're looking for anything that might give us a clue to his identity. Where he had dinner. How he knew Elizabeth and the other girls he killed. Pretend you know who he is. Urge him to give himself in. And the list goes on."

"Is that how Mia handled it?"

"She tried. He didn't talk much after the first call.

He obviously knew we'd be listening in then and trying to track him."

"Were all his calls to my grandmother at night?" Helena asked.

"The first two were. The last one was on a rainy Sunday morning."

Barker turned to Hunter. "Anything else I should go over with Helena before I go?"

"Think you covered almost everything. I can take over from here."

Helena walked Barker to the door. Hunter took the opportunity to return a phone call to Natalie Martin, an extremely talented profiler on loan from the FBI.

As usual, Natalie wasted no time with small talk. "I've been thinking about our French Kiss guy's call to Helena Cosworth last night. I keep trying to fit him into a recognizable pattern based on his first three murders, but this whole phone call routine throws a monkey wrench into my efforts. Things just aren't adding up."

"Have you talked to anyone else on the team about that?"

"Not yet. I'm working on a new graph that I'd like to run by the whole task force later today. Can you set that up?"

"I'm not sure what everybody else has on their plate, but I'll see what I can do."

"Thanks. Keep me posted."

While he'd been on the phone with Natalie, he'd heard the doorbell and the deep, commanding voice of the team's unofficial, volunteer profiler.

Hunter assumed Barker had let him in before he left

since Helena was not supposed to be opening her door to a stranger. No doubt Antoine Robicheaux was already charming Helena's socks off. Hopefully, just her socks.

HELENA STARED AT the latest investigator to arrive— a hunk of a guy who Cory had briefly introduced as one of the team. Late thirties, raven-black hair with wavy locks that fell mischievously across his brow. Chocolate-colored eyes a girl could drown in.

"I suppose you're here to see Detective Bergeron," she said, ushering him through the door.

"If you're Helena Cosworth, I'm here to see you."

Hunter joined them in the foyer. "About damn time you showed up." His tone clearly indicated the anger wasn't real.

"If you'd told me an angel was waiting, I would have made it a lot sooner."

"Cool it, Romeo. Did Barker take care of introductions?"

"Only the basic," Helena said. "I'm not sure why Detective Robicheaux is here."

"To clear that up, Robicheaux isn't a detective," Hunter explained. "He's former FBI with the best success rate in the country for apprehending serial killers."

"All true," Robicheaux said.

"I forgot to mention modesty," Hunter joked.

"And you must be Mia Cosworth's beautiful and talented granddaughter," Robicheaux said. "Your grandmother raved about you constantly."

"She was a bit biased in my favor. How did you know Mia?"

"I did all her security work for her. Set up the gate system a few years back. Planned a new and more secure system that my company was about to install for her when she had her fall. I wish there would have been something I could have installed to prevent that."

"So do I. Exactly what were you planning to install?"

"Mia wanted improved digital control pads with security cameras at the gate and she wanted personal pass codes for every apartment. That way, she could change a tenant's apartment code when they moved out instead of changing to a new code for everyone."

"I guess that makes sense," Helena agreed. "I'm not sure that now is the best time to tackle that. I just put the property up for sale."

"It'll increase the value of the property significantly in the current fear crisis. And it will keep you and your tenants safer. But, up to you."

"I'll think about it."

"While we're at it, you should consider replacing the courtyard lighting system with motion sensors that include hidden cameras."

"I suppose you do all of that, as well."

"My security company, Guardian Safe, does all that and more and we do it better than anyone else. We've provided bodyguard services for many sports and entertainment stars as well as foreign dignitaries. Never a screwup."

"That's impressive."

"I'd recommend you put a few hidden cameras in the house, as well."

She wasn't ready to go that far. "No hidden cameras inside my house. No spy equipment of any kind. In fact, I need to think about all of this and go over it with my Realtor before I agree to your recommendations."

One of her phones was already being wiretapped. She wasn't about to trust someone nicknamed Romeo or anyone else to hide cameras inside her house. Next thing she knew, instead of her artwork being on the internet, it would be her boobs and bottom.

"The woman has spoken," Robicheaux said. "The original workups for security improvements are in my car along with a list of recommendations and price estimates. I'll leave them with you."

"I'll walk out with you to get them," Hunter said.

Helena said her goodbyes and went back into the kitchen. She'd been back in New Orleans only three days and she felt as if she were losing total control of her life.

She wondered if Mia had felt the same helplessness when she started receiving the killer's phone calls and Hunter had taken control of her life. Regardless, she must have fully trusted Hunter to give him the gate code and a key.

Hunter returned a few minutes later, rolled-up blueprints and a large brown envelope in hand. He sat them on the kitchen counter.

"If there's anything here you don't understand, you can give Robicheaux a call. I'm sure he'll stop back by and go over the security additions in more detail."

"I just need time," Helena said. "Everything seems

to be coming at me at once. This is a far cry from the ordered, peaceful life I'm used to."

"A life I'm sure you miss and can't wait to get back to."

She couldn't deny that, but she'd never let Hunter know that a huge part of what was making this so difficult was being with him.

Time to change the subject. "Did you bring the recording of Mia's calls with the monster?"

"No. We'll need to go down to the precinct for me to play them for you. That is police policy when dealing with this type of homicide."

And then she'd need a drink. She was a train wreck now. She might freak out completely when she heard those calls.

Chapter Eight

This was Helena's first visit to a police precinct. Dozens of people were crowded into tight quarters, most working in individual cubicles or small private offices. The rest were in groups, engaged in conversation in the open space or clustered around one of the cubicles.

She noted that over half of the offices and cubicles were empty. That made sense. The real police work was undoubtedly done on the streets.

Hunter led her through a maze, acknowledging a few people with a nod or a small wave. He stopped at one office with an open door and introduced her to Lane Crosby, a lanky man with heavy facial hair who looked to be in his midforties, and Natalie Martin, an attractive brunette woman about the same age.

"Do they know why I'm here today?" Helena asked as the continued down the maze of small offices.

"They do and neither of them think it's a good idea, though Natalie Martin does have some ideas for discussion that center around the phone calls you're getting. That's one reason I wanted Barker and Natalie to at least meet you."

"Do you think saying hello changed their mind about my listening to the calls to Mia?"

"No, and I didn't expect it to. But it's a start. They're concerned about any information leaking out at this crucial stage in the investigation. The more people who know the facts we've kept under wraps, the more likely the press will pick up a leak and run with the info. It's their job, of course, but sometimes it makes it harder for us to do ours."

Hunter stopped at a door near the end of the hall and opened it with a key.

She stepped inside. The room was barely big enough for a rectangular conference table and the eight folding chairs huddled around it. A small, professional grade player was already set up at the end of the table.

"Are others joining us?" she asked.

"No, it will be just the two of us, but we're short on private meeting space." He pulled out a chair for her. "Take a seat and we'll get started."

"Will we be listening to a tape or a digital recording?"

"Digital. We'll start when you're ready, but we can stop at any point to talk about what you've heard or to give yourself a break to recoup."

"If it's that bad, the most difficult part may be knowing that Mia had to listen to it."

"She was always cool. It was almost as if she enjoyed her part in going after this monster."

"I wouldn't know since I was kept out of the loop, but I never knew her to back down from a challenge."

"She would have made a terrific law enforcement

officer," Hunter said. "Missed her calling. She'd probably be running the whole FBI now."

"Don't expect the same from me," Helena assured him. "Dealing with killers is positively not my calling."

"You're hanging in there pretty well so far." Hunter took the seat catty-corner from hers at the end of the table.

"Just as a reminder, we don't have a record of their first conversation since no one saw that one coming. All we have is the report from her as to what she remembered. I don't have that with me, but I've read it enough times, I almost have it memorized."

"Can you brief me on that before we get started?" Helena said. "That will give me a better sense of how the conversations flowed."

"Basically, the first contact was a meet and greet moment."

"Which means?"

"He called her by name and noted that she'd been very busy and successful in raising funds to help get him arrested. He insisted that he wasn't the monster she described him as. Told her he had no more control over his murders then she did over her breathing. And then he threw in a few gory details, some in French."

"He sounds insane."

"He did on the subsequent calls, too."

"What else did he say on the first call?"

"He hoped they could become friends and that she shouldn't go to the cops. Then he stressed he wasn't afraid of the cops because we were too stupid to see what was right in front of our faces. That's pretty much the opinion of criminals in general—that is until they get arrested."

"Did he threaten her?"

"Not other than an implied threat that if she talked to anyone in law enforcement, she would pay dearly for that mistake."

"So, I'm guessing Mia immediately called 911?"

"No. She immediately called me."

Hunter Bergeron to the rescue. Mia's calling him almost felt like a betrayal to Helena except that it had likely been the smartest thing to do.

"I think we've covered call one," Hunter said. "The other two will be much shorter since he was no doubt avoiding our tracking the call and showing up to arrest him."

"He seems to be well versed in how these investigations work."

"He got better at it as he went along. Are you ready to start the machine?"

"As ready as I'll ever be."

She sat up straight in her chair but clasped her hands in her lap. Hunter punched the play button.

"Call two."

"Hello."

A chill struck bone deep when she heard Mia's voice. It was almost as if Mia was speaking to them from the grave.

"*Bonjour, madam.* Have you missed me?" The voice sounded male.

"A little. Why did you wait so long to call?"

Mia was definitely playing along with him. Obviously, she'd been coached on how to handle the calls. She sounded amazingly calm.

"I know you hate me, but you don't know the real me. You think I like killing?"

"Don't you?"

"It's more like an obsession. But there were memorable moments, like when I helped her out of her red silky panties."

"I don't want to hear about panties. I think you want to turn yourself in."

The phone clicked, the connection broken.

The machine kept running.

The third call was in a female voice. "What was your father like, Mia?"

"He was a good and loving man. Was yours?"

"He was a cowardly wimp, let my stepmother walk all over him. I hate wimps."

"You need help. I can get it for you."

"No, but I'd love to meet your granddaughter. I hear she's beautiful. Will she be visiting soon?"

"Don't ever mention her again."

"I won't. It's time to move on. *Aide de Dieu.*"

Helena shuddered as the connection broke. *Aide de Dieu.* God help. "What did he mean by that?"

"We're not sure. Mia fell four days later. We investigated thoroughly. Like I said before, no sign of foul play."

"How close did you come to actually tracking his location through the phone calls?"

"Not close enough nor fast enough to ever see him or talk to anyone who had. We can verify that the calls were from somewhere within a sixty-mile radius of the French Quarter."

"And he never contacted anyone about the other murders?"

"If he has, none of them have shared it with the police."

"There must be a reason he contacted Mia and no one else. Maybe Mia was right and it was a cry for help."

"I think it was far more likely he was just running scared because she had everyone talking about him and searching for him, all looking to collect the sizable reward money. She's not here now, so he's taking it out on you."

"All that reward money and yet he still hasn't been apprehended," Helena said. "So, he might actually be criminally insane and yet brilliant."

"He's smart, but we'll get him eventually," Hunter said. "The challenge is arresting him before he kills his next victim. That's why we've got so many men working this full-time."

"And why you don't get to eat or sleep on a regular basis?"

"Yeah. I didn't mean to crash on your couch in the wee hours of the morning. I just closed my eyes and that was it."

"No problem," she said, though it had been. It had set off a chain of desire and arousal that threatened her shaky control.

"If that's all you have, let's get out of here," she said, suddenly eager to be out in the sunshine and with enough people that hopefully an incidental touch or a sympathetic word wouldn't set her off again.

Hunter unplugged the listening device and wrapped the cord. "What do you have planned for the rest of the day?"

"I thought I'd give Alyssa a call and see if she's free for lunch."

"Good idea. Both of you need a break from this garbage. I can drop you off at her place or drop both of you off at the restaurant of your choice."

"Sounds good."

She placed the call while Hunter waited. Alyssa seemed pleased at Helena's invite, and suggested they have lunch at the Napoleon House, a favorite French Quarter spot of almost everybody who spent any time there. Plus, it was within walking distance.

After getting off the phone Helena saw no reason not to mention her plans for the evening since Hunter insisted on knowing every move she made.

"I'm having dinner tonight with Pierre Benoit."

He frowned. "Why?"

"He invited me, and I owe him a dinner."

"I ask again. Why?"

"He kind of walked me through some of the legal entanglements in settling Mia's estate. He seems like a nice guy. What is it you have against him?"

"Other than that he's arrogant and rude?"

"I haven't found him to be either of those things. For the record, he doesn't seem to be any fonder of you than you are of him."

"What's he complaining about?"

"He says you harassed him and went overboard with your interrogation. Not in those exact words, but that was the drift."

"I did my job."

"Did you consider him a suspect?"

"I considered everybody a suspect until I could prove they weren't."

"Then he's no longer a suspect in your eyes?"

"He had opportunity and the ability, but no motive. And he has an ironclad alibi, though I never fully trust those, either."

"What about Connor Harrington?" she asked, not sure why he popped into her mind so quickly.

"He checked out, along with everybody else who I could link in any way with Elizabeth. I thought for a while we might have a credible online suspect. Turned out the supposedly college freshman she was hot and heavy with on a chat site was eighty-five and lives halfway around the world." He opened the door and they started down the hallway. "Where are you and Mr. Personality going to dinner?"

There was no way to miss the satire. Could it possibly be that Hunter was jealous of her going out with Pierre? If he was, the emotion was six years too late.

"Pierre mentioned a new French restaurant in the Garden District he wants to try."

"Nice. Somewhere you can swallow slimy snails."

"Says a man who sucks the heads on crawfish. Besides, I like escargot."

"Touché. I'll still need the name of the restaurant."

"I'll be with Pierre. I'm sure I won't need a body-guard."

"Never trust a Frenchman."

"Your last name is Bergeron. You're French Creole."

"Exactly."

She shook her head at him and struggled to keep from smiling. He could always make her laugh—until the day he'd left her drowning in tears.

She quickened her pace and didn't slow down until they were back in Hunter's car.

Hunter picked Alyssa up on the way and let them out near the front door of the restaurant.

They requested a table in the back corner, so it would be quiet enough to talk.

"You can't imagine how glad I was to hear from you," Alyssa said as soon as the hostess walked away.

"Is anything wrong?" Helena asked.

"Possibly, and it concerns you."

Chapter Nine

The look on Alyssa's face emphasized her dismay. Helena had no idea what was coming next.

"Do you remember that tourist I told you about, the one whose resemblance to Elizabeth Grayson is absolutely uncanny?"

"Lacy?"

"Right. I had a dream about her last night."

"I'm not surprised, considering how upset you got when you met her."

"She wasn't by herself in the dream," Alyssa said. "You were with her."

"Definitely a nightmare," Helena said. "I haven't even met her."

"I'm sure it was you," Alyssa explained. "You and Lacy were running through a swampy area, tripping on underbrush and ducking tree branches."

"Why were we running?"

"To get away from the man who was chasing you."

"The same unidentifiable man with a knife?" Helena asked.

"Yes. The bloody hunting knife was identifiable.

I'm not a medium," Alyssa insisted again. "But it sure seems like the universe is trying to tell me something."

Helena reached across the table and laid her hands on top of Alyssa's. They were icy cold.

"I can understand why you're upset, Alyssa, but this is likely your subconscious reacting to all the talk of the serial killer and seeing someone who reminded you of Elizabeth."

"I know that, but the nightmare seemed so real."

"Have you ever correctly predicted a dangerous event?"

"No. Except..."

"Except what?

"Twenty years ago when my six-year-old sister drowned in a neighbor's pool. I saw her floating under the water one night in a dream. She was smiling up at me peacefully. Six days later she was dead."

Chills ran up Helena's spine. She understood Alyssa's fear of dreams and her own imagination a lot better now. "Is that the only time you had a dangerous premonition that came true?"

"Pretty much. I mean I can frequently tell when a woman is cruising for trouble with a lover or job, but that has more to do with what she tells me and how she says it. That comes from years of practicing."

"I know you're worried about me and Lacy, but you've got to leave this in the hands of the police. I'm not in danger. Neither is Lacy. Hunter Bergeron and the NOPD are making certain of that."

"Intellectually, I know that," Alyssa agreed. "There are cops everywhere in the French Quarter. Uniformed and plainclothes. Walking. Driving cars. Some even on horseback. But…"

The waitress came to take their drink order.

"I'd like a glass of chardonnay," Helena said "How about you, Alyssa? A little alcohol might calm those ragged nerves."

"Can't hurt," she said. "I'll have the same."

Alyssa didn't exactly relax, but after two glasses of wine, a large bowl of seafood gumbo with toasted baguette slices and an hour of avoiding any talk of the French Kiss Killer, they managed to find a few things to laugh about before they said their goodbyes.

In spite of her assurances to Alyssa, Helena found herself turning back more than once on the walk home to make sure she wasn't being stalked.

BY 6:30 THAT EVENING, Helena had showered, glossed her lips, applied a light coat of mascara and did what she could to tame her hair—which wasn't much in this kind of humidity.

She pulled her favorite, slightly revealing little black dress from the closet and slipped into it while her mind replayed her last two phone calls of the afternoon.

Thankfully, both were on her new, private phone and not from the phantom caller.

The first call had been from Beth Macon, the owner of the Boston gallery where Helena would start work in November. Beth had sold one of Helena's favorite paintings for seven thousand dollars.

The amount was dizzying to Helena and several thousand more than she'd ever made on one oil painting.

She'd celebrate with a glass of good champagne tonight with Pierre Benoit. At least they'd have something pleasant to discuss.

She was truly starting to dread their evening though it had little to do with Pierre and all to do with her. It would be hard to be congenial with a guy she barely knew when her life was trapped in a tangled, murderous web.

The second call had been from Beverly Ingram. She still had no inquiries about the vacant apartment. That was a first since the apartments had always been in such demand.

Location. Location. Location. In the heart of the French Quarter. A beautiful courtyard and tons of atmosphere. The shadow of a serial killer hanging over it like a shroud.

Helena unzipped the travel jewelry bag she'd brought with her and chose a favorite pair of silver hoop earrings. She slipped out of her comfortable flats and into a pair of red, strappy sandals with nosebleed heels.

A quick turn in front of the mirror and she decided she looked nice enough for an expensive French restaurant. Or for dinner at the Aquarelle Hotel. Considering that option immediately improved her level of enthusiasm.

She'd have a much better chance of running into Lacy and her friend there and get to see for herself this remarkable likeness that Alyssa kept talking about.

This was what her life had been reduced to. Rather than enjoying a nice dinner with a handsome attorney who might even be fun, she was more excited about a murder investigation and chasing someone else's nightmares.

She picked up her phone and made a quick call to Hunter. He answered on the first ring.

"What's up?"

"Change of plans."

"Dumping Pierre? Smart move."

"I'm not dumping Pierre. Change of restaurants. We're going to the Aquarelle Hotel if I can get reservations at this late date."

"Ask for Connor Harrington. He'll get you in."

"I'll try that, and I'm telling you this because you asked, but I don't need or want someone to follow me around town. I promise we'll stay on the safe, beaten path."

"Got it. You're on your own. Have fun. Seriously, do have fun. You deserve a break."

He didn't sound a bit jealous this time. She should be happier about that.

PIERRE SEEMED TO resent her discarding his suggestion for a restaurant without checking with him first. She refused to feel too bad about it. After all, it was going to be her treat, though she expected him to protest that, at least half-heartedly.

He wouldn't win. This was a payback for a favor, not a date. Dates required more emotional capital than she could afford right now.

She glanced around the room as the hostess showed them to their table but didn't see anyone she recognized. Unlike the bar last night, the dinner bunch was a reserved group, mostly middle-aged or older.

A very attractive waitress stopped by their table. "Can I get you a cocktail?"

"I'll take a Glenlivet over ice," Pierre said.

Nice and pricey. He probably figured he earned it with his free legal advice. Perhaps he had.

"And for you?" the waitress addressed Helena.

"A glass of celebratory champagne," she said. "What do you have that's nice but reasonable?"

"We have a very good Moët & Chandon."

"Sounds perfect."

Pierre didn't ask what she was celebrating, and she'd just started to tell him about it when he started reading her the menu. When he got to the lobster and filet mignon, he paused.

"That sounds really good if they know how to grill a decent steak," he said.

"You can always send it back if it doesn't meet your expectations."

"Believe me, I've had to do that many times in other restaurants," he assured her. "What are you thinking about? The stuffed trout and the blackened redfish both look like good choices if you're not up for lobster."

"I'm thinking about the avocado and crab salad."

"A salad. That's it? You're celebrating inheriting a fortune in the city with the best food on the planet. You should spring for the most expensive item on the menu."

As he had.

"I inherited an estate but lost a beloved grandmother," Helena said. "That's not something I can celebrate."

"I never knew my grandparents, but I can see why you might feel that way," Pierre said. "How's the new job in Boston working out?" he asked, smartly changing the subject.

"Quite well, though I don't start until the first of November. With luck, I'll have sold the carriage house property by then."

"Then you'll be not only wealthy but beautiful and talented. Men will be falling at your feet. I can't imagine why some lucky guy hasn't grabbed you up before now."

"I'm not partial to men who grab."

He smiled. "I put that badly, but you know what I mean. Come to think of it, I'm good friends with Kelly Abby who owns a gallery in the Warehouse District. She's recently divorced and thinking about moving to California. She might be putting her shop on the market. You could buy it and immerse yourself in the art world without leaving the New Orleans area. I'm sure you could sell a few paintings if you owned your own gallery. There's probably a lot less competition here."

As if she wasn't talented enough to compete with the best. Okay, maybe Hunter had a point after all. Pierre was a bit arrogant.

Conversation came easier after they finished their drinks. They were halfway through dinner when three stunning women, all who appeared to be in their early- to mid-twenties, walked into the restaurant. Few eyes didn't follow them as the hostess led them to a table near the back of the restaurant.

Helena saw the woman who must be Lacy and felt a tightening in her chest. Same hair color and style as Elizabeth. The same thin, willowy build. The shape of the nose was slightly different and Lacy's lips were not quite as full. Those were the types of minor details few except an artist would notice.

Not identical, but close. No wonder she'd thrown Alyssa for such a loop.

"That looks like three women out for trouble tonight," Pierre noted.

"They just look like young women out to have a good time on their vacation to me."

"What makes you think they're on vacation?"

"Just a hunch."

Only one of the three might be the undercover policewoman that Hunter had mentioned. If so, she was indisputably good at her job. Helena assumed she was the one who looked slightly older than the others, but she couldn't be sure. Only Lacy stood out.

She noticed Pierre staring at the women and kept expecting him to say something about the likeness. He didn't, though he had to notice. Perhaps he didn't want to upset Helena. Not mentioning it was upsetting her more.

Helena moved her salad around with her fork while Pierre finished chewing his last bite of steak. Finally, she gave in to temptation. "Does the blonde in the group you said were looking for trouble remind you of anyone?"

He wiped his mouth on the white linen napkin while he studied the young women. "Seems like I may have seen her before. Is she a movie star or one of those supermodels who pop up on all the magazine covers?"

"She's not famous that I know of. I just think she looks a lot like Elizabeth Grayson."

He shook his head. "Don't tell me you've already contracted the bug."

"What bug is that?"

"Serial killer addiction. It's been a little over six months since Elizabeth's murder and that's all anybody is talking about these days. As if we don't have shootings on a regular basis like every big city."

"It's different," she said, without explaining how.

"Sorry," Pierre said. "It's just getting to the point you can't have a conversation in this town that isn't saturated with fear and gore. Frankly, the girl in the sundress that barely covers her buns could be Elizabeth's body double and I wouldn't know it. I don't think I ever met Ella's great-niece but once."

But he had noticed the slightly daring length of Lacy's attire.

Helena was only half finished with her huge salad, but she'd lost her appetite. Pierre changed the subject to brag about a divorce case he was working on where he was destroying the philandering husband and his well-known attorney.

A few minutes later, Connor walked in. She watched him as he scanned the dining area, looking extremely pleased by the number of customers. He crossed the room and went straight to the table occupied by Lacy's party.

She could tell from the familiar way they greeted each other that they'd met before—only natural since he was an important member of the hotel management team.

The restaurant was almost full now. It was a safe guess that many of the people in the restaurant had witnessed the entrance of three women who were young, beautiful and sexy.

The elusive serial killer could be one of that number. He could be any man in this restaurant, or perhaps even a woman.

Sitting unnoticed. Following his victim and plotting her death or searching for his next victim.

Not murdering by choice but ordered to by some inner demon that ruled him.

Her insides quaked, and she couldn't wait to get out of there, even if all she had to look forward to was a possible phone call from a demented killer.

HELENA HAD JUST slipped out of her shoes and dress when her phone jingled. She reached for the phone. The text was from Hunter. Unwelcome but pleasurable anticipation zinged through her senses followed by a quick burst of dread that it might be bad news.

Target practice tomorrow morning. Pick you up at ten. Wear something comfortable and shoes you can walk in. Slather on the sunscreen. I'll bring the mosquito spray.

Before she could answer or even digest that message, another text came through.

Doing this as a friend and not a cop, so you can turn me down if you want. I'd rather you didn't.

The thought of holding a gun made her nervous. The idea of pulling a trigger tightened knots in her stomach. Yet deep inside, she knew if it came to saving her life or someone else's she could do it.

There was a time when Hunter hadn't found even killing in self-defense palatable. Her thoughts traveled back to the night their relationship took its first nosedive. The first time Hunter had killed someone in the line of duty.

He'd rung the doorbell here at the carriage house in the wee hours of the morning. She'd rushed to the door in her pajamas. One peek through the door's peephole and she'd known that something terrible had happened. She'd unlocked the door and swung it open.

Sweat had pooled at his armpits, staining the shirt of his uniform. The muscles in his jaw and neck were stretched thin, the lines in his face pulled tight, blue-corded veins seemed to stitch his face together. His eyes had a wild fire in them that she had never seen before.

Her initial fear had been that he'd been shot, but there was no blood. By that time, Mia had reached the door and had the composure to pull him inside.

It had taken several minutes for him to get the story out. He and his partner had taken a domestic abuse call at a small house near the edge of the Quarter. By the time they arrived, the argument appeared to be over. He was short on details as were the news reports the following day.

The bottom line was that two people ended up dead in an investigation he and his partner didn't take seriously enough. The woman was shot by her husband. The husband lost his life to a bullet from Hunter's gun.

That was the first night Hunter had spent the night on the same couch he'd slept on last night, once again leaving without waking her.

The next morning, he was suspended without pay pending further investigation of the incident. The day after he turned in his resignation and stopped by her house briefly to tell her that he was no longer with the police force.

She'd pleaded with him to talk things over with her, to let her help him get through this. She'd be there for him always. She loved and believed in him with all her heart.

He'd told her how much he loved her. She had faith things would all work out. Their wedding was two days away. The wedding that never happened.

Somehow, he must have gotten his act together over the following six years. He'd done it without her help.

She changed into a flowing lounging gown and stepped out on the balcony. There was no breeze, just layers of thick, stifling humidity.

The area was deserted except for three young men walking down the opposite side of the street, to-go cups in hand. She was about to step back inside when a car pulled up and stopped. A woman jumped out and slammed the door. She staggered away, obviously drunk or maybe drugged. The car followed at the same speed.

Panic hit as thoughts of the serial killer pounded inside Helena's head. "I'm calling 911," she screamed.

The woman stopped and looked up at Helena. "Stay out of this, bitch." Her voice was so slurred the words were barely distinguishable.

Helena got the message. The thanks for being a Good Samaritan. Still, Helena ducked back inside and retrieved her phone. When she got back to the balcony, the car was parked, and the young man was holding the woman's head as she threw up on the street.

When she finished, he pulled a handkerchief from his pocket and wiped her mouth. They stood there in the moonlight, his arms around her protectively, her head resting against his chest.

When she'd steadied, he led her back to the car and helped her inside. Before he climbed behind the wheel, he looked up at Helena and waved.

"Sorry about the noise," he called, in a voice that showed no sign of drunkenness. "Her twenty-first birthday. One too many hurricanes. I've got her. She'll be okay."

False alarm but the fear lingered. There was a killer out there somewhere. Someone who knew both her and Mia. Likely someone who lived in the French Quarter. Possibly someone they knew well and who had known Elizabeth Grayson well.

Someone the young victim would have trusted and

gone with willingly. At least that seemed to be the most credible theory. Someone who had killed four times and gotten away with it.

Helena got ready for bed, but with little hope of falling asleep quickly. Counting sheep had never worked for her, so she looked up at the ceiling, watching the dancing shadows of the fan's whirling blades.

Eventually, her traitorous thoughts crept back to Hunter and the way he'd looked sleeping on her sofa last night. Impulsively, her hands slid down her abdomen and touched the hairy triangle between her legs.

She imagined they were Hunter's hands, exploring, finding all the right places to drive her crazy. Lost in desire, she brought herself to pleasure but knew that would never be enough.

She wasn't over him. That couldn't be clearer. She needed closure or she would never be able to move on and love again.

Even if it sent her into another spiral of heartbreak, they had to talk about the past.

Chapter Ten

Helena slipped a pair of worn sneakers into the bottom of her flowered tote bag. Hunter had specified comfortable shoes, so she'd be prepared if she needed them. In the meantime, her cute flat-heel sandals with ties at the ankles did great things for her ankles and thighs.

Her white shorts, off-the-shoulder teal-colored top and reliable silver hoop earrings finished the look.

What was she thinking? The last thing she wanted was to incite a seduction scene.

She checked her closet and pulled out a pair of loose-fitting cargo pants and an olive green cotton T-shirt that looked far more appropriate for shooting pistols or shotguns or whatever type of weapon Hunter had in mind.

The gate buzzer sounded as she finished dressing. She glanced at the clock. Only 9:30. Too early for Hunter. Besides, he knew the code. This is where cameras at the gate would come in handy.

"Can I help you?"

"Hi. It's Robicheaux here. Did I catch you at a bad time?"

"Not exactly, but I'm expecting Hunter any minute."

"We can make this quick. All I need is about ten minutes of your time to go over some modifications my tech team suggested. Not that I'm pushing, but I want you to have all the options before you make a final decision."

"Okay. I'll buzz you in."

He was at her door in minutes.

She opened it and welcomed him inside. Once again, there was no escaping his incredible good looks and masculinity. Odd that she was entirely aware of that and yet felt none of the heated, heart-stopping attraction she felt when Hunter stepped into a room.

"Is that coffee I smell?" Romeo asked.

"It is. Would you like a cup?"

"Wouldn't turn it down."

He followed her back to the kitchen. While she filled his cup, he spread the revised notes and blueprints on the table.

"I hear you and Hunter are going down to bayou country today."

"He only mentioned shooting lessons to me. I'm pretty sure it's a losing cause. I've never even held a gun and I'm not enthused about starting now."

"You may change your mind once you get the hang of it. It can be addictive. Even if you don't like shooting, you are in for a real treat. You'll love Eulalie."

"Is that a person?"

"Barker's mama. When her husband died, she moved back to her old family home on a bayou southwest of town. She runs a B and B and gives swamp tours."

"She does sound fascinating," Helena agreed. "At least the day won't be a total loss."

"If you get tired of paper plate targets or tin cans, you can shoot a water moccasin or two."

"Now I'm excited. *Not.*"

"You should get Hunter to take you exploring in one of Eulalie's pirogues. Elizabeth Grayson's crime scene is just a short ride down the bayou from the B and B."

This whole shooting idea sounded more bizarre by the minute. Why would Hunter take her anywhere near the murder scene? Surely there were shooting ranges right here in town.

"Speaking of Elizabeth, did her killer contact you again last night?" Robicheaux asked.

"How do you know about the first call? I thought that was highly confidential."

"I'm in the official loop. After the French Kiss Killer's third victim was found, Hunter got permission to call me in as a volunteer adviser to the task force."

"I didn't realize that."

"Yep. So far, I've been very little help. The killer seems to be dealing the cards and we're trying to figure out how to play them. The guy's smart. No one's denying that."

Robicheaux went over the modifications with her while he finished his coffee.

"Any questions?" he asked.

"Not at the moment."

"In that case I've probably taken up enough of your time this morning. Enjoy the rest of your day with Hunter. Who knows when he'll get another day off?

I got a hunch the infamous serial killer is puckering up for his next kiss of death."

HUNTER ARRIVED SHORTLY after Robicheaux left. She still thought it strange they were driving out of the city for target practice when he didn't even have time to eat or sleep on a regular basis.

The good news was that Hunter seemed more relaxed on the ride down to Eulalie's than he had since she met him. This might turn into the perfect time and place to seek closure, although any serious reckoning about their past would complicate working with him on the killer's phone calls.

They crossed the Crescent City Connection, the wide cantilever bridge that separated New Orleans from the area known as the Westbank. Forty minutes later, they turned onto a gravel road and she spotted a wooden sign that read Eulalie's Swamp Tours and B and B with an arrow that pointed to the left.

Hunter took the first quick left next to three wooden mailboxes perched atop rusting metal posts.

"It's difficult to believe anyone lives in an area this isolated, much less runs a business."

"Out-of-state tourists love this kind of atmosphere for a swamp tour. But don't fret. The house is comfortable and once you taste Eulalie's cooking, you'll never want to leave."

"It sounds as if you come out here often."

"Every chance I get, which hasn't been much lately. The only reason I can make it today is that my supervisor ordered me to take a day off. Claims I'm going to collapse in the middle of a shoot-out if I don't get some sleep."

"Which you're not getting."

"Actually, the sun got up before I did this morning. Haven't slept that late in weeks."

"Are your long hours tied to the serial killer investigation?"

"Not entirely. I still have to take my share of the department's homicide cases. But dealing with a serial killer who seems to schedule his strikes by the calendar has upped the urgency."

Which meant the odds were good that the killer might contact Helena again soon. For as long as the call lasted, discovering a clue to the killer's identity would depend solely on Helena's ability to guide the conversation. She'd never backed away from a pressure situation, but neither had she ever felt this unqualified to make the right decisions.

She tried to ease the enormity of that responsibility by studying the passing landscape. There was a scattering of trees, mostly cypress, and huge clumps of tall grasses in various shades of green. Bluebird and purple martin houses were plentiful. Large blackbirds sat on telephone wires. Several buzzards circled an area about fifty yards to the west.

They stopped at a fork in the hard dirt road. Signs indicated one way for the swamp tour and another for the B and B check-in. Hunter stayed left following the arrow to the B and B. Helena's mind slipped into artistic mode and began to frame a painting in her mind. A young woman walking through the tall grass. The woman would be small, the focus on the isolation. Deep shadows. Dark clouds.

A house came into view, breaking her concentration.

It was a small clapboard structure, set on stilts, with a railed veranda that circled the building. A set of wooden steps led to the covered porch.

"This doesn't look big enough to be a B and B."

"That's just the house," Hunter explained. "There are five small fishing cabins on the back of her property."

"Then the house is just where Euralie lives?"

"Only in part of it. She rents the two bedrooms and a shared bath on the back of the house. Her living quarters are the front half of the house. She claims she likes a cozy space."

Hunter followed the road to a graveled parking area to the left of the house. A big yellow mutt and a smaller black retriever came running to meet them from the far side of the porch. Hunter hunched over to greet and pet them. They responded with excessive licks and tail wagging.

"This is Captain," Hunter said, giving the yellow mutt a good ear scratching. "And the black beauty here is Bailey."

Helena took to the dogs instantly but quickly realized that she'd never seen Hunter interact with any kind of pet before. Another heartwarming side of him she didn't need to discover right now.

When their fingers accidentally tangled in Captain's long hair, a heated zing vibrated through her.

She pulled away and hurried to the steps that led to

the veranda. Hunter followed. The dogs went running off again. By the time they reached the porch, Eulalie was waiting for them.

She fell into Hunter's arms for a warm bear hug before she even bothered to look at Helena.

She looked younger than Helena had expected, around midfifties she'd guess. That made sense. Cory Barker was likely only a few years older than Helena.

Eulalie had an athletic build and long brown hair that she wore pulled back in a ponytail. She was dressed in a lightweight denim shirt over khaki trousers and sneakers, as if ready to take off on one of her swamp tours at a minute's notice.

No makeup but a nice tan and a great smile. She turned and flashed it in Helena's direction.

"Who's the *jolie femme*?" Eulalie asked.

"This is Helena Cosworth," Hunter said.

"Are you kin to Mia Cosworth?" Eulalie asked, switching easily from the Cajun expression for "pretty lady" back to English. Helena imagined the Cajun French that seemed to come so naturally to Eulalie was a hit with the tourists.

"Yes. Mia was my grandmother. Did you know her?"

"I never met her, but I saw her on TV when she was raising money to help catch that French Kiss maniac. I was so impressed with what she was doing to help, I made a small donation myself."

"I don't know what you're cooking," Hunter said, "but if it's half as good as it smells, it'll be wonderful."

Helena knew he was trying to change the subject

for her benefit. He wouldn't have known that Robicheaux had already told him how close they were to the crime scene. His effort to control the conversation didn't faze their hostess.

"Bad enough he killed that pretty young teenager, but he did it on my stomping grounds. Tell you one thing," Eulalie said, continuing her rant. "If I ever get my hands on that scum, he'll rue the day he ever came my way. I wouldn't feed him to the gators, though. They're too good for him."

"I agree," Helena said. And she had zero affinity for alligators.

"I was sure sorry to hear about your grandmother's fall," Eulalie said. "She looked in perfect health on TV and too young to be your grandmother."

"Thank you. I still miss her very much, but she had a good life, full of passion and joy. She'd be the first to tell you that."

"Sounds like you inherited her good spirit." Eulalie opened the screen door and motioned them inside. "Now how are you two connected? Cory said Hunter was bringing someone out to use the driving range today, but he didn't mention it was a female."

"We're old friends," Hunter said, as he followed Helena and Eulalie inside.

Old friends was definitely not how Helena would have described them.

"Lunch won't be ready until about twelve, but I got a mess of greens cooking on the stovetop and a pineapple-coconut cake baking in the oven. You should see the way Hunter can attack one of my cakes."

"I'm sure he can and will," Helena said, "but I hope you didn't go to all that trouble for us."

"Of course she did," Hunter teased. "And a good thing, too. If I showed up to an empty table, I'd swear I was no longer Eulalie's best beau."

"Listen at you go on. You know I don't play favorites with my guys. Spoil every one of you the same."

"How many do you have to spoil?" Helena asked.

"Well, it's mostly Romeo and Hunter here who Barker brings around, but he sometimes brings other buddies out here to shoot or fish. Now you two just make yourself at home while I stir up a fresh skillet of corn bread. Can't have greens without corn bread."

"Take your time," Hunter said. "In fact, I was thinking Helena and I could get in a little target practice before we stuff ourselves on your home cooking."

"You go right ahead. You know where everything is. Grab yourself a soft drink to take with you. You know where I keep them. It will get hot fast in the sun. I'll be tickled pink when that cool front they keep promising finally gets here."

Helena nodded. "I can't wait for that even if it does mean thundershowers."

"She's talking Louisiana cool, not Boston cool," Hunter said. "Don't get too excited or bother to put your shorts away." He walked to the door and called back to Eulalie. "Be back in about an hour."

Helena followed him down the outside steps. They

retrieved their soft drinks from a large black refrigerator just behind the red Jeep that was parked beneath the stilted house. The covered area seemed as much a catchall as a place to park.

There was also a pile of bricks, several large covered containers and a tire swing—rope attached—just waiting for a tree and a kid.

Hunter looked at her feet. "I hope you have some other shoes in that tote bag you brought with you."

"I have a pair of well-worn sneakers." She reached into her tote and pulled them out.

Hunter looked dubious. "I doubt those will keep your feet totally dry. Why not grab a pair of boots— or swamp stompers as they're known around here— from that large basket by the fridge. They're loaners for tourists who show up unprepared."

"Whatever you say, marksman."

"But shake them out first to make sure there's no spiders or scorpions waiting inside."

"On second thought, I'll just go barefoot." She didn't, of course. She could be walking through worse—if there was worse.

Helena checked out Hunter's footwear, hiking boots that could likely handle the worst of the swamp. She retrieved her sunglasses from the car while Hunter picked up his backpack and tossed it over his shoulders.

She walked beside him down a worn path that cut around the side of the house and off to the right. A few yards farther and the damp earth became even more soggy. She was thankful for the boots when the mire grew ankle deep in some spots. A fifteen-minute walk and they reached Cory Barker's famous shooting range. It exceeded her expectations.

"This actually is a gun range," she said.

"What did you think it would be?"

"Beer cans lining a row of fence posts."

"We started with not much more than that," Hunter admitted. "A couple of years ago, we pooled our monetary resources to upgrade a notch or two. Robicheaux put up most of the cash. He's making a killing in the security business."

"Yet he still volunteers to work with your task force?"

"Police work gets in your blood and he made a name for himself while with the FBI. He's even written a very successful book on getting into the mind of a serial killer. He's tried several times to get me to leave the force and go into business with him."

"Did you consider it?"

Hunter placed his backpack on a long cement table. His expression was strangely brooding, the depths of his gaze seeming to swallow her.

"It took years too long, but I'm finally in a place where I feel comfortable in my own skin," Hunter said. "I like where I am. I fit into this world. I feel like what I do makes a difference."

Hunter turned away quickly as if he'd said more than he meant to.

He lifted a petite, solid black pistol from his bag. It had to be for her, but she couldn't leave things this way. She might not like the answer to her question, but she had to ask it.

"Was needing to find yourself the reason you ran out on me, Hunter?"

Chapter Eleven

Hunter turned away and cursed silently. He'd said too much. He'd been afraid he'd have a weak moment like this if he spent too much time alone with Helena.

"This isn't the best time to talk about that."

"Why not? There's certainly no one around to hear it."

"The investigation is consuming me and delving into old emotions could put it and you in danger." That was neither an exaggeration nor a lie. But it was an evasion and he doubted she'd settle for that.

"I can take the truth, Hunter. I'm not looking for another chance with you or even an apology for the way you left. I just need to know why. Really why. Not the pathetic excuse that you gave about not being able to go through with the wedding."

He leaned against the shooting rest and searched his mind for the right words.

"I wasn't lying to you back then, Helena. Walking out was the hardest thing I've ever done, but I had too many inner demons I needed to deal with before I could be a decent husband. Marrying you then wouldn't have been fair to you."

"Do you think giving up on us without discussing those demons was fair to me? Was making me feel like our whole relationship was fake fair to me?"

He could hear the building anger in her voice, but it was tinged with sadness. He deserved the anger, but he couldn't let her turn on him now. Her safety was at stake.

"The decisions I made had left an innocent woman dead and a young boy an orphan. I had to find a way to live with that before I could face myself much less have anything worthwhile to offer you."

"It was self-defense, Hunter. The police cleared you of everything, only by then you'd resigned and left the area. Just one more question, Hunter."

He nodded, anxiety riding him hard as he dreaded whatever was coming next.

"Why did you bring me here today? That can't be a typical detective responsibility. Why did you go to the trouble to hook me up with Robicheaux and his security firm? We both know what we had died years ago, so why pretend like there's something special between us now?"

A relationship that died six years ago. That made it damn clear how she felt.

He reached for her hands and was shocked when she didn't pull away. "I care about you, Helena. I care a lot. I never stopped caring, but right now the most important thing is keeping you safe."

"You never called," Helena said. "In six years,

you never once called. That doesn't sound like caring to me."

"I called Mia several times to ask about you. She said I'd hurt you enough. You'd moved on and the best thing I could do for you was to stay out of your life."

"And you just took her word for that?"

"It made sense. I was stationed in Afghanistan. I watched friends die and worse. I wasn't sure I would get out of there alive. I had nothing to offer you. By the time I moved back to New Orleans, Mia assured me that you were a success and the last thing you needed was me raking up the past. I did what I believed was best for you."

When Helena looked up, her eyes were moist. "You and Mia were probably right. You broke my heart. I'm not sure there's enough of it left to try again even if we dared risk a second chance."

She wiped a tear from her cheek with the back of her hand. "I won't lie. There's still some chemistry between us but I don't know if I can ever love and trust you the way I did back then."

"And that's why all I'm asking now is that you let me keep you safe," he assured her. "Now, are you ready to learn how to use that pistol?"

"No, and I probably never will be, but since we're here, I'll give it a try."

He ached to take her in his arms, but she was right. They'd both gone through a lot in the past six years. They lived in two different worlds now and he couldn't see himself fitting into hers. One thing he knew for certain. He never wanted to fail her again.

HELENA FELT AS if she were caught in a whirlwind of emotions, so disoriented that she had no idea where she was going or why. She'd been searching for closure. Instead she'd been sucked inside an altered reality that bounced wildly in every direction.

She had no doubts about the strength of her sexual attraction to Hunter. Any lingering uncertainty disappeared the night he'd fallen asleep on her sofa. Her reactions to his smile, his touch, the sound of his voice made her dizzy with desire.

That had been true from the first time she'd ever laid eyes on him. True for her, but apparently not for him. Did she dare open her heart to him again?

If killing a man in self-defense made him run from his commitment to her, how could she trust that wouldn't happen again? He was still a cop. Was serving in the Marines enough to desensitize him to killing? If so, was that a good development?

If she let things go too far, if she made love to him, would she lose all ability to make anything close to a rational decision about their relationship? About their future?

Did she want to give up a new life in Boston to stay here with him? She definitely couldn't see him moving to Boston with her. He'd made it clear, he fit right here.

She shouldn't even be thinking about that. It was premature. They'd only just reconnected. But if she sold the house and moved to Boston, would she be giving up any chance of finding out if they could overcome the past and find real love again?

She struggled to push those questions aside and

focus on learning to handle the pistol that felt so foreign in her hand.

Her shooting skills showed no marked improvement over the following hour. She was more than relieved when Hunter suggested they'd had enough practice for one day.

Eulalie welcomed them back with her contagious smile and questions about their target practice. "If a ten-foot target is two feet away, I can probably hit it," Helena said.

"She was better than that. She was even opening her eyes when she pulled the trigger by the time we finished," Hunter teased.

"It takes a while to get comfortable with any kind of weapon," Eulalie assured her. "You'll get the hang of it. Having respect for a weapon is smart."

"Actually, she did exceptionally well for someone who'd never held a weapon before," Hunter bragged.

"And someone who hopes to never shoot one again." Helena walked over to where Eulalie was lifting catfish fillets from the skillet of hot grease.

"That looks and smells great," she said, eager to change the conversation from guns to food. "What can I do to help?"

"You can put some ice in the glasses for tea if you want?"

"I'd love to."

"Hunter, would you check that corn bread? It should be done."

"I'll be happy to." He opened the oven. "If it's black on top, does that mean it's ready?"

Eulalie looked over his shoulder and checked for herself. "That's golden brown and perfect. You mess with me, I'll take this spatula to your bottom and you know it."

"You can't talk that way to law enforcement."

"You just try me."

They were all laughing by the time the food was on the table. Eulalie had them bow for grace and then Hunter wasted no time digging in.

There wasn't much talking until they were all stuffed. They finished the meal off with cake that was as moist and delicious as any Helena had ever tasted. If she ate like this every day instead of her usual lunch salad she'd have to get longer brushes to reach her easel.

"You women have had a busy morning," Hunter said. "I'll do the gentlemanly thing and clean up the kitchen while you two go relax or take care of the swamp tour business if needed."

"I don't have but one tour scheduled this afternoon and my helper Evan is handling that. Won't take me but a minute to clean up the kitchen, and if you get more than one person working in that tiny space we'll be bumping into each other."

"And I'm only one person," Hunter said, "so that's why my offer stands."

"I have a better idea," Eulalie insisted. "You should show Helena around the area. Take the pirogue and give her a personal tour."

Hunter started stacking the dessert plates. "Have you ever been on a swamp tour, Helena?"

"Not since I was about ten years old when Mia thought it would be a capital idea. It wasn't. The tour guide got out of the boat, waded to a patch of dry land and picked up a baby alligator. He got back on the boat and handed it to me. I had nightmares for years about the mother alligator coming after me."

"I leave the gators alone," Eulalie said. "They don't bother me. I don't go getting them all riled up. You can trust Hunter to keep you safe. Cory's been bringing Romeo and Hunter up here to fish and hunt for years."

Robicheaux's words came to mind. At the time, Helena had thought visiting the bayou near where Elizabeth had been killed was the last thing she'd want to do this afternoon. Now the idea intrigued her.

She needed to know as much about Elizabeth's killer as she could before he called again. The more she knew, the better her chance at helping to bring him down.

"A personal tour sounds like a good idea if Hunter has time."

"Are you sure?" Hunter questioned. "We'll likely see an alligator or several."

"Alligators won't bother you," Eulalie said. "They aren't aggressive unless you try to hurt them or their babies."

"Which I definitely won't do," Helena said.

"All right then," Hunter said. "If you're game, I'm in."

The bayou was a fifteen-minute walk, due south from the B and B. Again, she tugged on the swamp stompers.

Within five minutes, she was thankful for them no

matter how unbecoming they were. The earth became squishy beneath her feet. A few yards more and an inch or two of standing water greeted every footfall.

The feeling of isolation was overpowering. Helena spooked at every rustle of the tall grasses and the branches above her. She imagined slithering snakes, rats, giant spiders or even scorpions crawling inside her boots or up the legs of her trousers.

Finally, they approached the muddy banks of the murky bayou. The waterway was wider than she expected, a good fifteen feet across at this point. She had no idea how deep it was since the dark murkiness of the water prevented her from seeing anything below the surface.

Scrawny cypress trees canopied the slow-moving water. Crows cawed as if warning they were invading their space. She startled a stately gray heron who took flight.

Helena scanned the area for a pirogue without luck. She did see what was left of a gray, deteriorating cabin with a partly missing tin roof a few yards down the bayou. It had apparently once rested on stilts, but it was leaning so badly now that the one weathered chair that leaned against the front wall looked as if it would collapse if sat in.

Helena took a couple of quick steps to catch up with Hunter. "Please tell me no one lives in that disaster."

"No, not for years, anyway. It's survived strictly from Eulalie's occasional intervention."

"Why would Eulalie want to save it?"

"It's a hit with the tourists, especially the young-

sters. They get excited when she has one of her work-
ers dress in a pair of ripped and faded overalls and sit
in that warped chair. Her handy man Joe Bob is especially popular. His wiry white beard and corncob pipe
don't hurt any, either. He waves, and the tourists snap
pictures like crazy."

"Sounds like a production."

"Like nothing you can imagine," Hunter said.
"When Eulalie starts telling those old Cajun tales
about growing up on the bayou and wrestling alligators with her grandpa, she has them in the palm of her
hand. Plus, she always locates a few alligators for them
to take pictures of so no one leaves disappointed. It's
hard to be out here very long without spotting a gator."

"In that situation, I prefer disappointment." She
scanned the area again. "Where is the pirogue you
talked about?"

"Just a few feet away." Hunter disappeared into a
cluster of thick brush and cypress trees. Once he was
out of sight, an eerie fear gripped her, and she was almost sorry she'd agreed to this.

And yet if the theory was correct, Elizabeth Grayson had willingly come with a killer who'd brought her
to a scene much like this one.

Or had she been forced here, screaming for help
with no one to hear her, by the monster who was now
trolling Helena by phone?

Helena struggled to push that image from her mind
as Hunter approached with a narrow, flat boat on his
back.

"Let me help you with that," she called.

"No need. It's not heavy, just awkward."

"Is it safe to leave a pirogue just stashed in the swamp?"

"It can't walk off by itself, especially when it's chained and locked to the trunk of the biggest tree around here. Not likely to get stolen, anyway. If you got here by bayou as most do, you have your own boat."

"Makes sense. What can I do to help?"

"Hold this rope so the dang thing doesn't go floating off without us while I get the pole and paddles."

Minutes later, they were floating deeper into a world that a lot of Louisianans had only seen in pictures and movies.

"Glad you suggested this," Hunter said. "No place is as soothing and peaceful as this. Listen to those tree frogs. That's as calming a serenade as you can get in any concert hall."

Soothing and peaceful were not the words she would have chosen, but it felt far less intimidating with Hunter so near.

A snowy white egret looked up from its fishing stance on the bank of the bayou and watched them float slowly by. The only time Hunter used a paddle was to steer them away from an occasional clump of vegetation that clogged part of the waterway.

They came to a fork, a wider stream of water opening up to their right. Hunter steered the pirogue straight ahead.

"How do you keep from getting lost out here?"

"I've been down here enough with Barker that I could probably navigate these waters in my sleep."

"What do you do down here?"

"Duck hunting is great in these parts. Good fishing, too, if you know where to go. Frogging is fun and good eating."

A splash to her left made her jump. She turned to see a large dog-sized rodent join a few buddies in the water."

Helena shuddered. "Are those rats?"

"Nutria, but basically they are large rodents. They're a real nuisance in these parts. They tear up the banks and cause unnecessary erosion."

"Don't the alligators eat them?"

"Yep and so do some people—no one I know, but a few adventurous souls."

Helena gagged. "I doubt I could ever eat again if I looked down and saw one of those giant rats on my plate."

"I'm with you. Check out the snake slithering across the water in front of us."

She sucked in a gulp of muggy air. The snake was at least five feet long and black or at least it looked dark-colored in the water.

"Please give it lots of room," she said.

"That's just a water snake. It won't hurt you. You gotta watch out for water moccasins, though. They make terrible company."

"Thanks for sharing that with me."

"Just pointing out the facts. No need to worry when I'm around. I do know how to shoot."

"Do you have a gun with you now?"

"Unless I'm asleep or making love, I'm toting. Even

then the weapon is within arm's reach. It goes with the job."

Helena felt something on her neck and swatted a large mosquito.

"Had enough?" Hunter asked.

She'd had more than enough, but she wasn't quite ready to go back. "Is this near the place where Elizabeth was killed?"

Hunter paddled them past the snake without even glancing at it. "So that's why you wanted to come out here. Sometimes Romeo talks too much."

"I get phone calls from a serial killer, Hunter. I think I can handle a crime scene."

"The two don't actually equate, but fair enough. Evidence indicates Elizabeth was killed and dragged into the bayou about ten minutes from here by boat."

"Then she didn't drown?"

"Are you sure you want to hear the gory details?"

"I'm a big girl. I can handle the truth, I think. Stop if I start to lose my lunch."

"The body was found not far away, tangled in the roots of cypress trees, but according to forensics she was already dead from slash wounds on her chest before she landed in the water."

"Were all four of his victims killed near here?"

"No. Just Elizabeth. The others were killed in Algiers swamps."

"Why do you think he changed his crime scene for Elizabeth?"

"We're not sure, but the killer made several changes in his modus operandi for Elizabeth. Look, I know you're tough, Helena, but I don't think we should take this conversation any further. What sounds like objective facts in the middle of the day can become fodder for nightmares when the sun goes down."

"I'm merely trying to get a handle on what my caller is truly capable of doing. It's hard to believe a man could function and pass himself off as human in the real world with that much evil in his heart."

"The bright side of all of this is that most people are truly good and have never even considered what it would be like to take someone's life."

"Yes, but I'm starting to understand how Mia became so fascinated by the workings of a serial killer's mind."

"Your grandmother had amazing insight. I swear she might have figured out who the killer was if she'd gotten the chance to talk to him a few more times."

"Don't count on that happening with me."

"I'm not."

Hunter paddled for a few more minutes before taking a fork to the left. He laid his paddle beneath the seat and took out the long pole to help guide him through some heavy vegetation that almost totally clogged the waterway.

"The crime scene is just to your right. Take a quick look while I turn the pirogue around so that we can start back."

"I don't see any crime scene tape."

"It's been six months and several tropical storms ago."

"Then how can you be sure this is the exact location? Everything we've passed seems almost the same to me."

"There are lots of landmarks. You just have to know what to look for."

He pointed to a garden of cypress trees. "That bald cypress is one of the tallest trees in this area. If you look in the top branches, you'll see the nest of a Southern bald eagle."

"You're right. I see it."

"What you can't see from the water is that there is an old logging road that runs almost to the bayou. We believe that the killer may have brought her here via that road instead of by boat. Easy in, easy out, for him."

"If he drove down here, couldn't you match tire tread?"

"We might have garnered a clue if we'd gotten here before heavy rains washed them all away."

The murky water rippled as Hunter slid the paddle beneath the surface and began to turn the small pirogue around. This time she didn't object.

Before they reached the B and B, Hunter got a call that he was needed back at the precinct ASAP.

There had been a foiled abduction in broad daylight in the French Quarter.

The killer may have attempted to strike again.

Chapter Twelve

Hunter dropped Helena off at home and went directly to the hospital where Cory Barker was waiting for the medical staff's permission to question today's victim. He found Barker in the hospital cafeteria nursing a cup of coffee.

"Still waiting, huh?"

"Yep. The nurse has my cell phone number and she promised to text me the second the doc says I can talk to his patient—Celeste Fountain. In the meantime, I decided to come down here, feed my need for caffeine and touch base with the crew handling the even stickier parts of the investigation—like locating the suspect."

"I talked to Lane Crosby on the way here," Hunter said. "He's questioning the two men who came to her rescue. He says the way they describe it, this was a purse snatching that went badly when she fought back."

Barker sipped his coffee from a disposable cup. "Coffee's out of a machine since the cafeteria's not open for dinner yet, but it's not too bad. Want me to grab you a cup?"

"Not yet. What's your take on the situation?"

"I figure we'll have the suspect in jail within twenty-four hours, but he's not the French Kiss Killer unless he's having a mental breakdown. Every move in today's attack was careless or downright stupid."

Hunter nodded. "Which is why we need to arrest today's would-be abductor as soon as possible and keep the hype that he might be the French Kiss Killer to a minimum."

"You're right," Barker agreed. "But wouldn't it be a roaring shocker if it turned out he was our guy?"

"Yep," Hunter said. "Be nice if I won the lottery tonight, too, but I won't start spending my winnings just yet."

Barker got a text from the nurse and the two of them headed to Celeste Fountain's third-floor hospital room. The doctor was standing outside her door to greet them. He introduced himself, then pulled off his glasses and slipped them into the pocket of his white coat.

"Mrs. Fountain has only minor injuries, a few bruises and scratches on her hands and knees. Nonetheless, she has been through a very traumatic experience this afternoon. She's convinced that she barely escaped a serial killer."

"We have no evidence of the serial killer aspect," Barker said. "But witnesses verify she was attacked in a public parking lot by an unknown assailant."

Hunter took a step in the direction of Celeste Fountain's room. "The most important thing right now is for us to get a description of the suspect so we can get him off the streets."

"She understands that," the doctor said. "Just don't push her too hard."

"Definitely not," Barker said.

The doctor left. The nurse ushered them into the victim's room and introduced them. The first thing Hunter noted was that Celeste looked nothing like Elizabeth or any of the other victims attributed to the serial killer.

Her hair was straight and coal black. She appeared slightly overweight and wore excessive makeup especially around her eyes.

Barker pulled a hand-size recorder from his pocket. "Do you mind if I record our conversation? I have a rotten memory and worse handwriting."

"I want to be recorded," Celeste said. "I have important things to say." She pushed a button and raised her bed until she was in a sitting position. "Are you going to read me my rights?"

An odd question. "We don't need to," Hunter explained. "You're the victim and we don't suspect you of doing anything wrong."

"I didn't," Celeste said. "I was just getting out of my car to go to my job."

"Where do you work?" Hunter asked.

"Well, I wasn't exactly going to my job. I got fired last week. I was going to look for a new job. I heard the Aquarelle Hotel was looking for waitresses and I've had lots of experience at that."

"For the record, can you give us your name, age, address and phone number?" Baker said.

She did. She was twenty-eight, divorced, the mother of a three-year old daughter who was currently in the father's custody. She lived in Gretna, a small town in the Westbank area.

"Take your time and tell us exactly what happened," Hunter said.

The gist of her explanation was that she had just parked and was getting out of her car when a slow-moving black sedan drove past her. She thought nothing of it since she figured he was looking for a parking space.

"Did you get a good look at the driver when he drove by?"

"Not the first time, but I saw plenty of him when he drove by again, that time at a crawl. He stopped right by me and lowered his window a crack like he had something to ask me.

"I couldn't hear what he said, so I approached his car."

Barker stepped over to the head of her bed. "What happened then?"

"First thing I knew, he jumped out of the car and grabbed me. I started screaming for help and the driver pulled a large black gun. He aimed it at me and told me to shut up or I was a dead woman."

This was the first Hunter had heard that a gun was involved. "What did you do?"

"I started kicking and scratching at his arms and face like a wildcat. I was scared but I'm no pushover. If he was going to shoot me, he'd have to do it in that busy parking lot."

"Did he try to force you into the car?"

"He didn't have time. Two young men heard the

commotion and came running. Dirty coward saw them and shoved me hard to the concrete. Miracle he didn't run over me."

"Did the attacker take your handbag?"

"He tried when he shoved me to the ground. Like I said, I put up a fight."

"Describe the attacker for us," Hunter said. "Give us as much information as possible. Take your time."

Her description was detailed. She said he was about the same height as Hunter, which would have made the man about six-two. Around a hundred and eighty pounds. He had spiky black hair and was wearing ripped jeans.

Barker asked the right questions to keep her going. If her description was dead-on, it shouldn't be hard to identify her attacker from a mug shot.

"I'm the one who saw him best," Celeste said. "Those guys ran him off, but they didn't get a good look at him. You can't trust what they say."

"You are a great help," Hunter assured her.

"If you catch him, does that mean I get the money?"

"What money is that?" Barker asked.

"That hundred thousand dollars I'm supposed to get for leading you to that Kiss Killer or whatever you call him. It'll go to me, won't it? They said it on TV. A hundred thousand dollars to anybody who helped them catch the killer. They can't lie on TV."

That was a new one to Hunter. "You did a brave thing to fight off your attacker," Hunter said, choosing his words carefully. "We haven't arrested anyone yet, but if that guy you fought off turns out to be the serial killer, I figure you're entitled to at least some of that money."

"*All* of that money," Celeste emphasized.

This wasn't an argument he could win. "Do you think you can pick him out of a lineup?"

"I'd know that creep if I saw him coming from a block away."

They stayed with her another thirty minutes. Hunter had no doubt they'd apprehend her abductor and zero confidence he would be their French Kiss Killer.

But he'd been wrong before.

HELENA SAT ON her balcony in one the two semi-comfortable chairs that went with a bistro set Mia had bought for her years ago. She sipped her white wine while her mind struggled with the shooting range conversation she'd had with Hunter.

Six years was a long time. So long, she'd almost convinced herself she'd moved on. She'd survived the heartache and become stronger and wiser for it.

In many ways, she had moved on. She'd finished her education, spent a year in France studying under an elite watercolorist. She'd taught a fine art class at Boston U and worked as a museum curator in a famous museum.

Now she'd sold a painting for seven thousand dollars. That was next to nothing compared to the estate that Mia had left her, but it had special meaning. Someone thought her painting was worth it and wanted it to hang in their house or office.

But no matter what strides she'd made, she'd never

wanted a man more than she wanted Hunter. She couldn't imagine that she ever could.

Passion raged inside her, a hunger for him so strong she felt it in every cell of her being. If anything, it was stronger than it had been before he'd run out on her.

She'd been caught up in a dream of forever with Hunter. He'd been twenty-five then, the same age she was now. A cocky young cop who took her breath away the first time she saw him patrolling their neighborhood.

She and her college friends blatantly flirted with him while he tried to avoid them like any good cop would. Eventually the chemistry overpowered him, too, and he agreed to go with her to an art show at Tulane where she was a freshman.

Back then there had been no dreams of making it big in the art world. No thoughts of Boston. Her idea of success had been showing her work at local galleries and teaching art at the high school level.

She still loved New Orleans. The money from the estate was enough to open her own gallery, though it wouldn't have the clout of the gallery she'd be working for in Boston.

Would she be willing to give up the new dream to take a chance on a man who'd walked out on her once before? Would she ever regain the trust she'd lost when he'd dumped her with no credible explanation for his leaving?

A piercing ring interrupted her troubling thoughts. It was her wiretapped phone, which meant it was Elizabeth's killer again. She shuddered, then jumped from her chair and rushed into the bedroom to answer it.

"Hello."

"Hello, my sweet."

The childish voice ripped through her.

"I guess you've already heard. Some idiot made a huge mistake. Tried to steal my thunder. He'll pay for that."

"Who made a mistake?"

"A nobody in a parking lot. Doesn't matter except he screwed up my timing with his foolish behavior. It's full speed ahead now. You should kiss Hunter good-bye."

"How did…"

The connection broke.

An icy chill settled bone deep as the madman's confusing words echoed in her brain.

Was he calling Hunter an idiot? Was he planning to kill him? Why else would he say she should kiss Hunter goodbye?

Another ring of a phone, this one emanating from the cell phone *not* being monitored. She checked the caller ID and answered quickly, her pulse still racing.

"Hello, Hunter."

"Are you okay?"

"Getting there. You?"

"So angry it's rattling my brain. I can't believe that psychopath had the gall to call you and threaten me."

"You heard the call?"

"Barely. I was on my way to my car and being followed by a noisy pack of reporters when I felt the vibration in my pocket."

"Why the reporters? Is there a new development I should know about?"

"The woman whose attack I rushed home to investigate is insisting to the media that her attacker is the French Kiss Killer and when they arrest him, she wants all the reward money."

"Do you think it actually was the serial killer who attacked her?"

"Not one iota of evidence of that."

"I guess that's what the caller meant by an idiot stealing his thunder."

"It's difficult to understand what's going on in his sick mind, but I figure he's mad that his fearful public may think he was the one who fouled up the abduction attempt this afternoon—if it actually was an abduction attempt."

"But you are convinced it wasn't him?"

"Close to certain, but we haven't identified a suspect as yet."

"But he said I should tell you goodbye." Her voice trembled. "He must be planning to kill you?"

"Don't worry, Helena. I plan to see that he doesn't. He's not going to hurt you, either. I'll see to that. There's a cop watching your house and gate right now. Go back to enjoying your wine on the balcony."

"But who is watching out for you?"

"My buddies Smith & Wesson."

"Okay, but I'm calling Romeo in the morning. No

cameras in my private spaces but the rest of his ideas are a go. If Mia could afford it, then I guess I can, too."

"Good thinking. Look, babe, I gotta run. Take care."

"Stay safe," she whispered. And then he was gone. No mention of when she'd see him again.

She had the horrible gut-wrenching feeling that it might be never.

ALYSSA SAT GLUED to her chair as the anchor on a rerun of the ten o'clock news gave details of an armed attacker trying to kidnap a young woman in broad daylight. The victim's name was being withheld but the assault had occurred only a few blocks from Alyssa's studio.

The victim was able to provide a detailed description of her attacker to the detectives, but the suspect was still on the loose.

There had been some speculation that the suspect might be the infamous French Kiss Killer, but that idea had not been substantiated by the NOPD.

She'd had a steady stream of customers from noon until she'd closed about thirty minutes ago. Several had mentioned concern about today's attack.

Alyssa backed up the feed and ran it again. Attack in the French Quarter—possible failed abduction. No one had died or been seriously injured. But someone could have been. Her heart pounded, and an eruption of acid pooled in her stomach. She ran for the bathroom, knowing she was about to lose her dinner.

The anxiety wasn't new. She'd lived with some level

of it ever since her first visit with Helena on Tuesday night. Meeting Lacy had only compounded the problem.

There was no logical explanation for her practically crippling apprehension, yet she couldn't shake it. She stood and walked over to the counter. Hunter Bergeron's card was still there where she'd left it when he'd come to talk to her about Lacy.

She glanced at the kitchen clock again. Too late to call, she thought, as she punched in his number, anyway. Her breath was coming hard and fast.

"Bergeron," he answered. "At your service."

"Hunter, it's Alyssa Orillon. I'm sorry if I woke you but this is sort of an emergency."

"What's wrong? Do you need an ambulance or a police officer?"

"Nothing like that. I just saw the evening news. I don't need the name of the young woman who was attacked this afternoon. Just tell me it wasn't Helena Cosworth or the tourist who looks like Elizabeth Grayson."

"It was neither Helena nor Lacy Blankenship. They're both safe."

Air rushed into Alyssa's lungs and she started to tremble. "That's all I needed to know."

She thanked Hunter and tried to assure him she'd be all right even though she didn't believe that herself.

There was only person who might be able to help her get past this. Her grandmother claimed she had lost all her psychic powers with age. Her memory was dimming, the distant past becoming more available than what she had for breakfast. But if anyone could help Alyssa understand what was going on, it was Brigitte.

The nursing home was across the Lake Pontchartrain Causeway, near where Alyssa's mother lived in Covington. It would take her at least an hour to get there in light traffic. It might be a wasted trip, but it was the only option she had.

The chances of it helping might improve if she could talk Helena into going with her. It was worth a try.

LACY SLIPPED HER magnetic hotel key into the slot, opened the door and tiptoed to her side of the bed. If she could wiggle out of her dress and bra, she might be able to slide beneath the crisp white sheets without waking her roommate. It was a long shot. Brenda was a very light sleeper.

But Lacy's lies were starting to become confusing even to her. She kicked out of her high-heeled sandals and twisted until she could reach the dress's back zipper.

"You don't have to sneak in. I'm not your mother."

"I woke you? Sorry, Brenda."

"I wasn't asleep. I worry when my best friend is out past midnight with a stranger."

"We're on vacation. Besides, he's not a stranger. He's a nice guy I've met several times."

"Ever heard of the French Kiss Killer?" Brenda asked sarcastically. "Everyone else in this town has. They say he's probably fun to be with, too, until he kills you."

"The odds of getting killed by a serial killer are lower than being abducted by an alien from outer space."

"You made that up."

"Sounds good, though, doesn't it?" she teased in an effort to get Brenda to lighten up.

"If you're not going to listen to me, then pay attention to our new friend Courtney. She lives in New Orleans, and she says never go off alone in this town with someone you don't know well."

"I didn't. I went off with a perfect gentleman who I've run into around the hotel several times. He didn't even try to put the make on me. How's that for class?"

"Oh, geeze. It's that guy who manages the restaurant, isn't it? No wonder he's always stopping by our table."

"Could be."

"I give up. You're going to do what you want to, anyway."

"And what I want is to spend the whole day with you tomorrow. How about visiting the Mardi Gras Museum?"

"I like that idea," Brenda said.

"Laissez les bons temps rouler," Lacy said as she sashayed to the bathroom to brush her teeth.

Brenda groaned. "Now you're speaking French."

"It's a Cajun expression for 'let the good times roll.' You gotta love this town."

IT FELT LIKE Helena had just fallen asleep when her alarm clock woke her with its piercing peal. She reached over to turn it off and realized it was her phone. She picked it up and read the time and caller ID display.

One fifty. Hunter.

"Hello."

"You sound as if I woke you."

"It is a wee hour of the morning," she said.

"Then I guess I should let you get back to sleep."

"Wake me up just to say goodbye? Nice try, Detective. Where are you?"

"Standing in front of your house."

"It's a little late for stalking me. There's room on the couch."

And here she went again, her body coming to life at the prospect of seeing him and possibly watching him do something as unremarkable as sleep. Her pulse raced as she pulled on her robe and ran down the stairs to let him in.

"You look beat," she said when he ambled through the door.

"Feel beat, too. Worse, I've spent every minute since I left here this afternoon running in frantic circles, chasing my tail."

"I take it that means you didn't arrest the parking lot villain."

"We can't even get a straight story on it. The victim says the guy had a gun. The young men who came to her rescue say they never saw it and that they had a good look at what was going on. The victim says he was trying to force her into his car. The same witnesses say he was trying to grab her handbag."

"The woman who was attacked should know," Helena insisted.

"She appears to have ulterior motives."

"Such as?"

"She claims her attacker was the French Kiss Killer, and since she described him to Barker and me, she deserves all the reward money."

"Did you explain to her it doesn't work that way? The info has to lead to the serial killer's arrest before there's a payoff."

"Yes, but I'm just one of those corrupt cops trying to keep the reward for myself or so she's complained to every reporter who'll talk to her. That's most of them."

"But you don't think he's the serial killer?"

"Nope, but we can't prove that until we arrest him. That reminds me. I'm supposed to tell you that Natalie Martin, the profiler on our team, wants to talk to you sometime today."

"Really? I thought your task force members didn't even want me to hear Mia's messages from the killer."

"Seems at least one of them is having a change of heart. Natalie has some ideas for how you can get more helpful responses and also keep the lunatic on the phone longer."

"I'm willing to meet with her, but from the way he talked tonight, that may have been his last call to me."

"Which would suit me just fine," Hunter said. "You've done enough."

"None of us have done enough unless we stop him before he kills again, and he sounds as if that is imminent."

"Again, that is not your responsibility."

Easy for him to say. "Exactly who is on the task force?"

"Detectives Cory Barker, Lane Crosby, Andy

George, Natalie and me. And then we have Robicheaux to call on when needed. We also have a lot of help from other guys in the department when the situation calls for it."

"If this goes on long enough, I guess I'll meet them all. Do you want something to eat or drink?"

"I could be persuaded. What do you have?"

"We'd best go to the kitchen and check it out. I haven't had a chance to grocery shop since I've been here. I'm still making do on the basics Ella bought for me before I arrived."

Hunter kicked out of his shoes and followed her in his stockinged feet. She went to the pantry.

He opened the fridge. "Ummm. Butter. Eggs. Creamer. And half a croissant. Can you top that?"

"I'll see you a loaf of wheat bread and raise you a box of tasteless-looking, healthy cereal," she joked. "Wait. I may have hit the mother lode. A small bottle of maple syrup and a box of pancake mix that says just add water. Pretty sure we have that."

"And I've discovered a half-pound package of bacon in the freezer right next to a pint of chocolate chip ice cream," Hunter said. "The makings of a feast. Can you cook?"

"No, but I can stir water into a box of mix."

"I'm impressed. I'm dynamite with a spatula," he claimed. He pulled one from Mia's utensil holder and twirled it like a baton before dropping it to the counter.

In minutes, the front of Helena's pajamas was sprinkled with the pancake mix. Hunter grabbed a dish towel and wiped it away. When his fingers brushed her nipples through the soft fabric, desire hummed through her.

What a difference a few hours could make. No, it wasn't the hours, it was all Hunter. Right after the phone call from the killer, Helena had felt as if she was on the verge of disaster, apprehension choking the life right out of her.

Hunter showed up and within minutes, the gloom had given way to teasing, laughter and the inevitable sensual tension. Cooking had never been this much fun. All the problems she'd been faced with earlier were still there, but they were coated with raw craving now.

Hunter defrosted the bacon in the microwave and then fried the slices until they were crispy, just the way she liked it. In between flipping her pancakes on the griddle, Helena brewed a pot of decaf coffee in case she ever got around to going back to bed tonight.

By the time they were ready to eat, the sensual tension was sparking like electricity. It was bound to lead to trouble. She dropped her fork while trying to take the first bite.

"Let me help you with that," Hunter offered. He speared a bite of his pancake, dragged it through a puddle of syrup and fed it to her. A drop of the warm, sweet syrup settled in the corner of her mouth.

She reached for her napkin, but not before Hunter leaned over and captured the syrup with his napkin. She felt light, frothy, as if gravity might not be able to anchor her to earth.

"I better get my own fork," she whispered, "or we may never get around to consuming our feast."

"Would that be so bad?" he asked.

She ignored the loaded question. There was no doubt in her mind that she was falling in love with Hunter again—if she'd ever been out of love. But this wasn't just love for the man he used to be, it was for the man he'd become. He was brave and confident, more sure of himself than when they'd been together. She'd never felt more protected.

But had he really changed? Was he capable of a forever commitment this time—if she got to that point herself? Or was she already there and only fooling herself?

Hunter devoured his food. She picked at hers. By the time they'd finished eating, her sensual excitement level had cooled but not by much.

It was late. Hunter had to be exhausted and who knew how much sleep he'd get before he felt compelled to get back on the job?

He insisted on helping her clean up the kitchen. He was rinsing the syrup from their plates when his phone buzzed. He picked it up. "Have to take this," he said. "Police work."

He set the plates in the sink and answered the phone as he walked out of the kitchen. She couldn't stop the thought from entering her mind—being married to a homicide detective probably meant a lot of nights of eating and sleeping alone.

But then being single did, too. She was used to that,

but she doubted any spouse of a cop ever got used to the dangerous risks.

"Good news or bad?" she asked when he rejoined her in the kitchen.

"Semi-good. Another witness who was also in the parking lot at the time of the incident called in with what he says is the suspect's license number."

"I'd think that deserved more than a semi-good," she said as she wiped down the counter.

"It would be except the witness mainly wanted to know about the award money, so the license number could be a hoax."

"Don't they know you'll figure it out quickly if they lie about something so easy to check?"

"I think they have so many dollar signs in their eyes, they can't see anything else. But it's a busy parking lot so it wouldn't be unusual for someone to see trouble and jot down the license number."

"Hopefully that's true in this case."

"I should be going," Hunter said. "Sorry I woke you, but I really wanted to see you tonight. I had to make sure you were okay after visiting the crime scene in the swamp and then dealing with that bizarre, disgusting phone call."

"I'm glad," she said. "It's late and you must be exhausted. The couch is still available if you want to crash there again."

"Sounds good." Instead of making a move in that direction, he walked over, poured himself another cup of coffee and sat down at the table. He looked serious and even a little apprehensive, which spiked the air with tension, no longer sensual.

"You asked me what happened to make me walk out on you just before our wedding."

Now she recognized the awkward aspect of the tension. It was dread.

"I wasn't completely honest with you," he admitted. "I think I owe you that."

So did she, but she wasn't sure she was ready to deal with the truth. "Was it another woman?"

"In a way, but not what you're implying."

"Then how?"

"I don't know if you remember, but I had killed my first person since becoming a member of the NOPD. Everyone assumed that was what had me so upset. They were wrong. My regret was that I hadn't killed him sooner."

"I know you were temporarily suspended, but then all charges were dropped when the shooting was ruled self-defense. I must be missing something."

Hunter stood and began to pace. "My partner and I were sent out to respond to a 911 call from an eight-year-old who said his daddy was drunk and was about to kill his mother. When we got there, the father came to the door. His wife and the kid were standing behind him."

Helena didn't interrupt. It was almost as if Hunter were no longer in her kitchen talking to her but had slipped back into a troubling past.

"The man had been drinking. The curses he hurled at my partner and I were slurred. He assured us there was no problem. He might have gotten a bit rowdy, but he would never harm his wife and boy.

"The woman backed him up, but we knew she was lying and so frightened of the guy she was shaking. She put her arm around the boy's shoulder and encouraged him to lie, as well.

"The boy insisted he made the call, but he knew his daddy wouldn't hurt them. His voice broke. Clearly, the kid was scared to death.

"I tried for thirty minutes to persuade the mother to press charges. She refused over and over, insisting they'd only been arguing and the boy had gotten upset. Finally, the man ordered us off his property."

"And by law you had to go?"

"By law and by policy, but even then, I'd turned around and was heading back to the house when we heard gunfire. We kicked in the door and found the man standing over his wife who he'd shot through the head. The boy was stretched out over his mother's bleeding body."

Tears filled Helena's eyes. No wonder that had hit Hunter so hard. She'd not known these details.

"You tried to save her," Helena said. "It was out of your control. The man must have still held the gun."

"He didn't," Hunter said. "He was unarmed. He'd tossed his weapon to the floor. When we burst through the door, the kid picked it up and pointed it at his dad."

Hunter stopped pacing but still avoided eye contact with Helena. "I couldn't let him do it. Not because I gave a damn about the man. My first impulse was to shoot him myself so the boy didn't have to live with that."

"But you didn't?"

"No. I jumped the kid and wrestled the gun from his hands. In the process, his drunken father was killed from a ricocheting bullet."

"No wonder you were hurting. I just wish you'd have told me that back then."

"I couldn't."

"Because you didn't trust me?"

"Because that boy was me, Helena."

Chapter Thirteen

Hunter's words made no sense to Helena. "I don't understand."

"I lived through that very same horror, except I was only six at the time. I called the police and then lied to them just like my mother told me to do. If I hadn't, he would have beaten both of us like he did almost every night, at least that's how it seemed to me then.

"That night he didn't beat her. Instead, he blew out my mother's brains. And then he came after me, beat me until I was unconscious."

"What happened to your father?"

"He went to prison. I never saw him again. I tried to find him when I finally started dealing with this after our breakup. He'd been released years before. He'd never come looking for me."

Things were starting to make sense and Helena's heart ached for the boy of six who'd faced such tragedy. But then she looked at the brilliant, dedicated detective standing in her kitchen and she knew he'd faced the worse and made it through.

"What happened to you after that?"

"I went from one foster home to another. Nobody let me stay for long. I had a giant chip on my shoulder and I was a troublemaker."

"Who later became a cop and then a Marine and is now a fantastic homicide detective."

"It took me years to get to this place. The problem was I never faced what I'd been through. I don't remember ever crying. I told friends at the new school I had to attend that my mother had died of cancer and that my dad was a fatally wounded war hero. The first time I remember weeping for my mother was the day I ran out on you.

"That's why I couldn't marry you then. I had nothing to offer you until I came to grips with my past. I had to prove to myself I could face the truth and move past it. I had to understand that I would never become the monster my father had been.

"As a kid, I had wanted to kill my dad and as a cop, I had wanted to kill the man who blew his son's mother's brains out. The past was destroying my future. I couldn't pull you into that."

"And you feel you've moved beyond that?"

"I do. It may sound corny, but the Marines did make a man of me. The intensive counseling I finally got helped, too."

She walked over and put her arms around his waist. "Welcome back, Hunter Bergeron. You were always that man to me."

He held her without talking for long minutes. "This is the real me," he whispered. "As good as it will likely ever get. Lots of faults, but I'm crazy in love with you.

Always have been. Always will be. No pressure, I just wanted you to know."

She had never loved him more.

"Now, does that offer still stand to sleep on your couch?"

"No. I don't think so. You're not couch material. But there's room in my bed for two."

HELENA CHANGED INTO a teal-colored satin cami pajama set in lieu of her flour-splattered ones while Hunter showered in her bathroom. The sliding doors to her balcony were already closed and locked; the heavy, noise-trapping drapes were pulled tight.

She plumped both their pillows and dimmed her bedside lamp to a soft glow. Anticipation swirled inside her, as she slid between the sheets.

The bathroom door opened, and Hunter stepped into the bedroom, only wearing one of her white, fluffy towels knotted at the waist. She stared at his broad chest as if seeing it for the first time.

In a way, she was. The ex-Marine at thirty-one was more muscular, his pecs and abs far more defined than they'd been the last time she and Hunter had shared a bed.

She thought his body was perfect then. Now he'd taken masculinity to a whole new level. If he didn't make a move on her soon, she'd explode.

He stepped closer to the bed then loosed the towel and let it fall to the floor. He was already hard, his erection proof that he was not too fatigued to feel the same desire that was vibrating through her.

Instead of climbing into bed with her, he lifted the top sheet and pulled it to the foot of the bed. She reached over to turn off the lamp.

"Please don't," he whispered. "Just let me look at you and drink all this in. You've walked through my dreams for six years, but it was never like this. You were never more beautiful, never more ravishing than you are at this minute."

She slipped her fingers beneath the spaghetti straps of the cami and slowly tugged them off her shoulders one at a time. Her breasts swelled above the fabric until she lifted the top over her head and tossed it to him.

"Want to help?" she tempted.

"I'm not sure I can and keep control."

Keep control. She was so caught up in the moment that she'd lost control. "I don't have any protection," she blurted out.

"I do," Hunter whispered, "though I haven't been intimate with a woman in almost a year. And only in my wildest dreams did I imagine a moment like this."

He removed a condom from his wallet and slid it onto her bedside table. Then without another word, he slid into bed beside her, raised up on one elbow and worked his hand beneath the elastic waist of her shorts.

His fingers brushed her coppery triangle of hair, finally dipping inside her. When she grew slick with desire, he slid the damp pajama shorts down her legs then twirled and shot them across the room.

He kissed her mouth, softly at first and then hard and relentlessly until her lips felt ravaged yet hungry for more. The kisses grew deeper still, stealing her breath until they both came up for air.

His hands cupped her breasts, his thumbs massaging her nipples before taking one at a time into his mouth. He nibbled gently and sucked until she moaned in voracious pleasure.

Then, trailing her abdomen with sweet kisses, his lips reached the erogenous area that took her to the edge of orgasm. Her body writhed and arched toward him.

He rolled away and raised on an elbow again. "I'm human, you know, and you're making it impossible for me to hold off until you're completely satisfied."

"I'm ready, so ready. I want you now. All of you."

He took a minute to encase his desire in the condom, then straddled her and fit his erection inside her. He thrust faster and faster, driving her delirious with desire.

Helena moaned and bit her lip, giving in to the thrill as they exploded together in savage release.

Hunter stayed on top of her for glorious minutes, his face flushed, his breathing coming in quick gasps. She closed her eyes, letting the perfection of the moment caress her soul.

"I love you, Helena Cosworth," he whispered, as he pulled her back into his arms.

"I love you, Hunter Bergeron." At that moment she knew she always would.

Hunter was soon fast asleep.

Helena lay awake, relishing the sound of his rhythmic breathing and the warm glow of her body after the loving.

The contentment was short-lived. Quivering tremors attacked in the dark as the killer's words came back to haunt her.

Please, God, don't let me have to say goodbye to Hunter or let him be forced to say goodbye to me.

The promise of happy-ever-after was within their grasp. *Don't let it be stolen from us now.*

SAYING GOODBYE ON a sticky note after the most memorable night of his life was a damned shame. Walking away from the bed where Helena lay sleeping was pure torture.

But he'd chosen this life and felt honored to be one of the youngest homicide detectives with the department. Having been named to head up the serial killer task force was lagniappe.

The task force was organized shortly after the third victim and gained momentum after Elizabeth Grayson's murder. They'd covered every angle, questioned hundreds of people, delved into the backgrounds of everyone who had a shred of evidence against them.

The killer had outsmarted them at every turn. He seemed to know what they were thinking before they acted. He was knowledgeable about their limitations within the law and made fools of them repeatedly, as he was doing with the repetitive phone calls.

They were desperate for a break and they may have just gotten it. Or they might be dealing with another kook.

Hunter finished writing his note.

Sorry I had to cut out like this. A new lead just in that might go nowhere. Don't go away. I'll be back. Love you.

It didn't even touch on what last night had meant to him. No room on the small paper square. No time to write it. Mainly, he'd never been good at putting his emotions into words.

He'd work on that.

He leaned over and let his lips brush Helena's. She stirred but didn't open her eyes. As much as he ached to crawl back into her bed and into her arms, he tiptoed away and left her sleeping.

HELENA WOKE TO a gentle ache in her thighs and heart-stopping memories rambling through her sleep-dulled brain. She rolled over and reached for Hunter. Her hand swept across empty sheets. The house was silent.

He was gone.

For a second she thought it might all have been a dream. And then she saw the yellow note attached to his pillow. She picked it up and flicked on the lamp.

She read the short note twice, hoping to find some hidden hint of how their lovemaking had affected him. "Love you" was as close as it got but she'd settle for that. She knew *love* wasn't a word he threw around carelessly.

The house seemed incredibly empty with him gone. Mia's absence magnified the feeling. It was as if the home where she'd spent so many happy hours was revolting against her.

After all, she'd come here to close this chapter of her past and turn Mia's beautiful house over to strangers.

Only houses didn't think or feel, and the real estate possibilities were at least temporarily in limbo. Besides, she'd be crazy to let anything distract from the ecstasy she'd shared with Hunter last night.

She stretched and luxuriated in the sensation of her nakedness against the sheets, reminding her of all the ways Hunter had explored and titillated her body last night.

The thrill of their lovemaking stayed with her through her first cup of coffee and shifted to anticipation for more of the same while she showered and dressed in a pale pink sundress with a halter neckline.

And then the dread and fear crept in, followed quickly by the urge to change into one of her painting smocks and take her easel into the courtyard. She needed an outlet for her joy and a calming for her soul.

Instead she decided to settle for taking a walk through the Quarter and stopping at Sophia's Bakery near her house for a chocolate croissant before the unforgiving heat claimed the day.

She waited until she was ready to walk out the door before making a call to Robicheaux and telling him she was ready to sign a contract for the proposed project. He made an appointment to meet at her house at three.

She started to call Hunter but hesitated. He'd ordered her not to leave the house without letting him know exactly where she'd be. On the other hand, she hated to interrupt him.

She decided on the latter. Better interrupted than

angry at her. Her pulse quickened as she punched in his number.

"Is anything wrong? Are you okay?" His usual greeting when she called. He was protective to the core.

"The only problem I have to report is that a sexy detective broke out of my house in the wee hours of the morning."

The comment was met with laughter. Lots of laughter. Her cheeks began to burn. "Was I on speaker?"

"Yeah. My bad. A group of us are in an online meeting with the chief. Speaker's off now."

"How's the new lead working out?" she asked.

"Too soon to say."

"That's better than 'nothing there.'"

"Yeah." He sounded distracted.

"Sorry that I caught you at a bad time," she said. "You said I should call when I leave the house so…"

"Where are you going?" he interrupted.

"For a walk around the neighborhood with a stop at the bakery. I don't need a police stalker. I just wanted you to know where I'll be."

"When are you leaving?"

"Right now."

"Wait ten minutes, and remember, no alleyways or shortcuts."

"I'll stay right here in the heart of the Quarter. I'll be fine."

"Okay. I'll call you later," he said.

He'd said okay, but she figured he'd still alert the cops in the area to keep an eye on her. As long as the killer was contacting her, she'd be considered high risk.

Her phone rang as she stepped into the courtyard. She closed and locked the door behind her and walked over to the fountain before answering.

"Hello."

"Is this Helena Cosworth?"

"Yes."

"It's me, Alyssa."

"Are you already up and working this early?"

"Up but not working. I'm taking the day off and driving across the lake to visit my grandmother. She's living in an assisted living center near my mother."

"Good for you. I'm sure she'll be glad to see you."

"You never know. Some days she's sharp enough to converse with me on almost any topic I bring up. Other days, she seems totally disoriented or not interested in anything I have to say. She'll fall asleep while I'm talking."

"How old is she now?"

"Ninety-two. But she drives her walker like a race car. The reason I called is that I'm hoping you'll ride over there with me."

Now things were starting to add up. "This wouldn't be the grandmother who used to be the famous medium, is she?"

"Yes, it's Brigitte, but I'm not counting on her advising you in any way. She claims her mind and body retired from all things psychic."

"Yet somehow, you hope she'll suddenly recover her skills and explain your bloody vision of me and Lacy?"

"I'm not expecting miracles. But what could it hurt to visit her?"

"No. I'm not going to pull a ninety-two-year-old woman into this. Please, let it go, Alyssa. You don't believe you have extrasensory skills yourself, so the visions are meaningless."

"You can ride out there to keep me company. If nothing else, you can meet Brigitte. She's a character worth knowing."

"I have an appointment here this afternoon at three with Romeo."

"With whom?"

"Real name, Antoine Robicheaux. He's a friend of Hunter's. Used to be an FBI agent but owns an apparently very successful security company now. Not sure if he's making me safe or a prisoner with all the locks he's installing, but the only way in for a criminal will be by helicopter."

"It would be cheaper to move Hunter Bergeron in with you."

"Are you staring into that fake crystal ball again?"

"Just a thought. But I'm serious about needing company on that long drive across the Causeway. If we leave here around eleven, we can easily be back by three."

"You're not going to give up, are you?"

"No," Alyssa said, "but I promise not to harp on the bloody images."

"In that case, I'll ride over with you."

"Great. Pick you up at eleven."

It was only half past eight now. Helena would still have plenty of time for her walk.

She heard her name called and looked up. Ella was

on her balcony, picking dead blooms from her Mandevilla plant and letting them parachute to the pebbled courtyard below.

"Do you have time for a cup of coffee?" Ella called.

Helena hated turning her down, but now she was primed for a morning walk and one of Sophia's flaky chocolate croissants.

"Why don't you come take a walk with me? I'll treat you to a cup of coffee at Sophia's bakery."

"I'd love to. Mia and I used to walk almost every day. I've tried doing it without her but it's not the same."

"I know. I miss her, too. Come on down. I'll wait."

There went her opportunity to do nothing but think of Hunter and the bizarre turns her life had taken over the past few days. But it would also help her avoid thinking of the killer and what he'd meant by his latest horrifying comments.

Ella was at the gate in less than ten minutes wearing a pair of athletic walking shoes, trousers, a colorful tunic and a large-brimmed straw hat.

"I sure do appreciate your asking me along," Ella said. "Sometimes I think I'll go bananas in that house thinking about poor Elizabeth. I can't even turn on the TV the past couple of weeks without hearing some reporter bantering about how it's right around the six-month mark and there's going to be another killing any day now. And I'm not just talking about the local channels, either."

"I'm sure it's been hard on you. All I can tell you is that the police are determined to make sure that the killer doesn't strike again."

"For sure, Hunter is," Ella agreed.

At seventy-two, Ella could still walk almost as fast as she talked and that was saying a lot. Several friends of Ella's and Mia's stopped to say hello. All of them were curious about what Helena was going to do with the carriage house and the adjoining property.

Helena had no answers for them. Hunter had told her he loved her. He hadn't said anything about the future. How could she make any definite plans without knowing where their relationship was heading?

The bakery was crowded when they arrived. She and Ella found a table for two near the left back corner but with a good view of everyone entering.

"This is the best people-watching area in the French Quarter," Ella said. "You see everything here. Look at that young woman who just walked in. Why in the world would she think having her hair two completely different colors would be becoming?"

"It's the style among the younger set," Helena offered.

"I suppose so. We didn't do that in my day."

The waitress stopped by their table and took their orders for coffee and chocolate croissants.

The bell over the door tingled again. Two young women stepped inside and scanned the area for an empty table before heading their way. Lacy and her friend.

It would be hard to bypass a catastrophe unless by some miracle, Ella didn't see the likeness between Lacy and Elizabeth. Only judging from Ella's pained expression, she already had. Her face was ashen as the young women found seats just two tables down from them.

"The blonde who just came in looks just like my Elizabeth." The timbre of Ella's voice was practically bloodcurdling. "You must see it, too."

"There's a likeness," Helena agreed. She reached over and took one of Ella's shaking hands. "This is making you uncomfortable. Why don't I have the waitress change our orders to takeout?"

"No," Ella said emphatically. "I'm not ready to go."

Helena couldn't believe sitting here and reliving the heartache of Elizabeth's death could be good for Ella but forcing her to leave could be even more devastating.

Lacy left her table after ordering and walked back to the restroom area. While she was gone the waitress brought Helena and Ella's order. Before Helena had time to stir cream into her coffee, two groups of women stopped by their table to say hello to Ella and Helena.

Ella barely spoke to any of them.

"Did you and Mia come in here often?" Helena asked when they were alone again.

"Every Tuesday and Thursday."

"You were a regular. No wonder so many of the customers know you."

"Mia knew and talked to everybody everywhere we went. Elizabeth was like that, too. I should have warned her more often not to trust strangers."

"Don't go blaming yourself, Ella. Elizabeth had a beautiful spirit. People young and old were drawn to her. That's all."

Ella was about to take a bite of her croissant when

Lacy sat back down at her table. The pastry slipped from Ella's shaky fingers and fell back to the saucer. A few drops of coffee spilled over Ella's fingers as she pushed the mug away.

"I'm sorry."

"Nothing to be sorry about." Helena dabbed up the spill with her paper napkin.

A few minutes later Connor Harrington stepped into the coffee shop. Judging from his clothing and sweat, he'd likely been to the nearby gym.

He went to the counter for a coffee and then headed toward Helena's table. He never made it. Instead he joined Lacy and her friend.

"Lacy and Brenda, a nice surprise running into the two of you," he greeted loudly enough for Helena to catch the friend's name.

In seconds he and Lacy were involved in an animated conversation. Brenda looked annoyed. Connor left a few minutes later with his coffee. He never noticed Helena or else he chose not to acknowledge her.

Ella continued to stare at her full cup of coffee and untouched croissant while Helena finished hers. "I hate to rush you, but I have an appointment at eleven," Helena said.

"I have no appetite today. We can go now," Ella agreed.

Helena paid the tab and left a tip.

Ella stopped next to Lacy as they were leaving and put a hand on the young woman's shoulder.

"I don't mean to upset you, dear, but you could be the twin of my great-niece who was murdered last spring."

Lacy looked perplexed. "I'm sorry."

"Nothing to be sorry for. You're beautiful. I only said this to warn you to be careful."

Lacy stared at Ella as if she was totally confused by the unusual comments from a stranger.

"Sure," Lacy said. "I'll stay out of trouble."

"Don't go off alone with anyone you don't know," Ella continued. "The serial killer who stole my niece's life may be looking for someone exactly like you."

Thankfully, Ella walked away after that. Lacy didn't say a word.

Her friend didn't stay silent. Brenda's words were loud and clear.

"If you don't heed Courtney's warning about hanging out with strangers, I don't suppose you're going to listen to that poor old lady who lost her niece, either."

Helena waited until they were outside before texting Hunter about seeing Lacy and Connor together.

Hunter's response was an emoji indicating he'd gotten her message. He was obviously busy, but Helena would have loved to know if Courtney was the undercover police officer who was supposed to be looking out for Lacy. If so, she might need to step up her efforts.

The killer's last phone call had warned he was moving full speed ahead.

Lunchtime for the residents was finishing up when Helena and Alyssa arrived at the assisted living center. Brigitte had finished her meal and was dawdling over a bowl of what looked like caramel pudding.

Brigitte seemed glad to see them and suggested they

go the center's atrium to talk, explaining that it felt almost like being outside but without the heat and humidity.

Alyssa offered to get her a wheelchair. Brigitte acted insulted. For good reason, Helena realized when they started walking. As promised, Brigitte was a Hells Angel behind that walker.

They stopped at a vending machine as they left the cafeteria and Alyssa got soft drinks for herself and Helena to tide them over until they had time to grab lunch.

"Are you sure you don't want anything from the machine, Grammy?" Alyssa asked.

"I'm sure unless they've added vodka."

"No vodka. I can get you an orange juice and you can pretend it's a vodka screwdriver."

"It's hard enough pretending you drove all the way over here in the middle of a work day just to chat. I'm sure you are looking for some type of interpretation."

Brigitte's wavery voice gave away her age as much as her wrinkles and nearly translucent skin did. On the other hand, her attitude and ease with words revealed she hadn't lost much in the intellect and wit departments.

But it was her extrasensory abilities they were about to put to the test. Helena grew more uneasy as Brigitte led them to a spot in the corner where three club chairs were placed around a small round table.

Alyssa brought up the subject of her frightening visions.

The only comforting aspect of this was that Brigitte showed no indication that she envisioned Helena splattered in blood.

Next, Alyssa spent a few minutes trying to engage Brigitte in small talk. Brigitte wasn't buying it.

Brigitte reached over and put a bony, vein-stitched hand on Helena's arm. "It's great meeting you, but I'm out of the psychic game. My brain and body won't hold up to constantly living inside other people's problems."

An odd way of putting it. Giving up the game rather than losing the ability.

"My sweet granddaughter here is much smarter than me. She's convinced herself she's a fraud so that she doesn't have to take on the responsibility of saving everyone around her. I pray she stays on that path, but today's visit makes me fear otherwise."

"I am a fraud, Grammy, except…"

She hesitated. Helena and Brigitte stayed quiet and waited on her to finish that pronouncement.

"Except that sometimes I let my imagination take off on its own and leave my reasoning ability behind. I don't trust what I see in my subconscious, but I can't always brush it off."

Brigitte leaned back in her chair and closed her eyes as if fading off to sleep. Helena felt terrible. They'd not only infringed on her peace of mind, they were interfering with her naptime.

A second later, she opened her eyes again and stared at Alyssa. "If you're here for me to interpret your imaginings, you're wasting all our time."

"We shouldn't have bothered you," Helena said.

"Alyssa, please don't say more about the hallucinations."

Brigitte went on as if Helena hadn't jumped into the conversation. "If you're here for advice, Alyssa, I'd warn you to trust your instincts. Go where angels fear to tread if you must, but don't bury yourself in regrets when you realize you haven't changed anything. The future is not in your hands."

Helena was awed by Brigitte's wisdom. As Mia had always said, the passing years might rob one of a few brain cells, but the lessons living taught more than made up for that.

"Don't you even want to hear about what I'm dealing with, what my friend Helena is facing?" Alyssa asked, disappointment bleeding into her words.

"No. It wouldn't help, Alyssa. Even when I was at the top of my game, I could never absorb meaning from secondhand interpretations. Talking about it is only going to upset all of us."

"I was hoping meeting Helena would spark your own vision."

"I'm sorry, sweetie. I've spent the past few years learning to block those revelations. Now, I don't know what exciting plans you ladies have for the rest of the day, but it's nap time for me."

"We'll walk you back to your room," Alyssa said.

"I'm not an invalid. You're my guests. I'll walk you to the door."

Brigitte was not one to argue with, so they followed as she led the way.

They shared goodbyes and hugs but for some reason Brigitte suggested Alyssa get the car and pick up Helena at the door.

The second Alyssa was out of earshot, Brigitte reached for Helena's hand. The calm Brigitte had exhibited inside the building transformed into drawn facial muscles and anxiety clouding her eyes.

Helena suddenly realized why Brigitte had sent Alyssa on without her, Brigitte was about to go herself where angels feared to tread. Helena was pretty sure she was not going to like what she was about to hear.

Chapter Fourteen

Helena waited in dread for Brigitte Orillon to speak her mind. She didn't have to wait long.

"I don't know what Alyssa saw or thinks she saw in her phantasms."

"She thinks someone is out to kill me, but she can't decipher who," Helena said, keeping it simple. "In any case, we were wrong to intrude on you like this."

"No. You were right to come. Alyssa is right about your being in danger."

"But you wouldn't let her talk about it."

"I needed to focus on my own reactions and I don't want her to get drawn into the danger. That can happen, you know. It's another reason I've never encouraged her to develop the gift and follow in my footsteps. Much better for her to think she has no extrasensory perception, though she clearly has a great depth of feelings."

"I understand."

"Listen close to what I have to say. Someone is coming after you, but you will not be his only victim."

"Who will be the second victim?"

"I don't know."

"Who is the man who wants me dead?"

"I don't know that, either. I sense what I cannot see, but his heart is as black as a moonless night and evil consumes his soul."

Alyssa drove up in the circular drive and stopped a few feet from them.

Brigitte squeezed Helena's hand. "Nothing is what it seems. Trust no one."

Helena's blood ran icy cold as she climbed into the passenger side of Alyssa's compact car. She reached into her handbag and fumbled for her phone. She needed to talk to Hunter, needed to hear his voice. Needed his strength.

But she couldn't say all of that in front of Alyssa and disturbing Hunter on the job wouldn't help.

Besides, Brigitte was ninety-two years old. What could she possibly know about the killer that Hunter and his task force, including his brilliant FBI profiler and past FBI agent Romeo, didn't know? Helena could not be in safer hands.

It was ten after three when Hunter and Barker walked out of the chief of police's office. The latest finding was newsworthy and the mayor was eager to share any good news having to deal with the serial killer. Unfortunately, it didn't mean they had an ID on the suspect who might strike again at any minute.

They had two hours before they had to be at the mayor's office for a press conference.

"One of us should call and give the news to Robicheaux," Barker said. "He'll flip if he hears the bombshell developments from the chief on TV before he hears it from us."

"He does like to be on the inside," Hunter said, "and he did call this right from the beginning—more or less."

"Yeah, yeah, I know," Baker said. "And I'm the one who argued he was wrong."

"You'll owe him a couple of beers for that."

"Speaking of having a drink, we don't have but two hours before we have to be back here. Do you want to grab a coffee and a slice of pie?"

"I would except I need to check in with Helena. Robicheaux is supposed to be there designing a new security system for her house and rental property. I can kill two birds with one stone."

"Things seem to be getting serious awfully fast between you and Helena. I know she's cooperating with the investigation and times are tense. Just remember that emotions can get all mixed up in the heat of danger."

"I've got my head on straight."

Not actually true. He'd never had his head on straight where Helena was concerned, but he wouldn't let his emotions interfere with his main focus—keeping her safe.

Nothing they'd learned today had decreased the danger. If anything, it may have upped it.

"I might as well tell you now, Barker. I haven't mentioned this to Helena or to anyone on the task force yet except Natalie Martin, but I've decided to block her from taking any more calls from the lunatic."

"Where in the hell did that idea come from? You know that as faulty and unsuccessful as that's been, it's our only contact with the suspect."

"He can still call. He just won't get through to Helena. I'll take the calls and I'll do the talking to him."

"Do that and he'll quit calling. You know we still have Elizabeth Grayson's killer out there. He's unhinged. The calls make that clear. He could strike again any day now."

"More reason I don't want her exposed to his threats any longer."

"I can almost guarantee you Robicheaux will balk at that idea. Even if he doesn't, it damn sure won't get my vote."

"Sorry, but it's not up for a vote. Helena is not bait."

"Okay. Your call, at least for now. See you at five."

"I'll be there."

There was a good chance Elizabeth's killer would be watching the breaking news bite that would be broadcast on every local channel and likely picked up by some twenty-four-hour news channels, as well.

With luck, he'd realize the odds were turning against him and decide to surrender.

Bad thing about luck was you simply couldn't count on it.

HELENA DIDN'T TELL Alyssa about her private conversation with Brigitte. Actually, the two of them had talked very little on the way home. When they were back on the south shore of Lake Pontchartrain, Alyssa offered to buy her lunch.

Helena was certain she couldn't hold down a spoon-ful of food. She took a rain check, claiming she had some tasks to take care of around the house before Robicheaux arrived.

There were no tasks and if there had been, Helena would have been too shaken to do them. Brigitte's words had upset her even worse than the monster's phone calls.

She'd never taken mediums or any kind of psychic phenomena seriously. It was ridiculous that she was so upset by it now. It was the constant living with the reality of a madman calling and possibly stalking her that had her beginning to accept the murderously inexplicable as truth.

Once inside the house, Helena walked through every room checking the locks on the few windows and doors that opened to the outside. Hunter had said there would always be someone nearby to hear her if she screamed for help. She was tempted to test him on that.

She took a deep breath and exhaled slowly. Her paranoia was getting out of hand. Nothing had changed. Hunter had promised he'd let nothing happen to her and she had no reason to doubt him.

Helena walked into what had been Mia's bedroom, crashed on top of the coverlet and chose a book from the stack of nonfiction crime selections. She opened it to a random page and began to read.

Common and not-so-common traits of serial killers.

She scanned the page. There was nothing unexpected or shocking in the list, but a couple of traits piqued her curiosity.

A desire to improve their expertise with every murder. A fascination with death and watching someone die.

She turned the page and found notes that Mia had entered on the margins from the top to the bottom of the page. One sentence stood out in her mind.

Be careful whom you trust.

It was the trust element again. Trust no one. Be careful whom you trust. How many times and in how many different ways had she heard that warning in the few days she'd been here?

The doorbell rang. She closed the book and returned it to the stack before hurrying to the door.

She hoped it would be Hunter. Instead it was Robicheaux.

"You look beautiful, as usual," he quipped once she'd ushered him inside.

"You don't look so bad yourself."

"Thanks."

He grinned at her compliment. She had no doubt he knew how handsome he was and made use of that in selling his security services.

"Glad you decided to go with at least some of the items we talked about," he said. "It's the latest technology— top of the line. Might not be as good as having a sharpshooter like Hunter hovering over you every second, but it doesn't snore."

"Ah, honesty in packaging."

"I do deliver perfection."

"Modest, too."

"When you're good, flaunt it. Speaking of that, I hear you're a terrific artist."

"Don't believe everything you hear. We should probably get down to business before you get me started on my art."

"Whatever you like."

His relaxed and flirty attitude made it almost seem the serial killer situation was faraway fiction. It felt good even though she knew the attempts at normalcy on both their parts was only temporary escapism.

"I know we discussed a lot of this already," Helena said. "But I need you to go over exactly what will be installed, the cost and how it works. Then I'll make a decision on which options I want to go with."

"Absolutely. Can we do this in the kitchen? It's easier if I can lay everything out visually for you."

"Sure."

He followed her to the kitchen. "Would you like something to drink?" she asked. "Coffee, iced tea, a soft drink?"

"What, no booze?"

"No hard liquor. I might be able to come up with a cold beer."

"I'll go with that and next time I stop by, I'll see your bar gets restocked. It's the least a friend can do."

She got a beer from the fridge and sat it in front of him while he laid out his multipage proposal.

"What made you leave the FBI for the security business?" she asked.

"I liked the idea of being rich. And the FBI has too many stifling rules that I never liked to follow."

"They must have been upset when you resigned. I heard you were a superstar."

"I think they were glad to see me go so that they could get a rule-follower in my place. And don't believe the superstar bit. That was more a case of being in the right place at the right time—more than once. Jimmy Gott Terlecki was a good example of that."

The name sounded vaguely familiar. "Who was Terlecki?"

"A serial killer who preyed on young strippers and prostitutes in the DC area just under eight years ago. I was following where the clues led when I caught him in the act of strangling a prostitute in the back seat of his car."

"Is he still in prison?"

"Never spent a day in prison. He pulled a gun on me. I was faster than him. I put a bullet through his head."

The doorbell rang. "That's probably Hunter," she said.

By the time she reached the door he'd already let himself in. He pulled her into his arms for a kiss that sent tremors of desire from her head to her toes. She felt relieved. And safer. She always felt safe when Hunter was nearby.

"Is Robicheaux here yet?" he asked.

"He's in the kitchen."

"Good. I need to fill him in on the latest developments."

"I guess that means you want privacy."

"No. You may as well hear this, too. The mayor,

chief of police, Barker and I are making a statement to the press at five."

Her pulse raced. "You've arrested the French Kill Killer?"

"The news is not quite that big, but it's positive."

In minutes the three of them had moved from the kitchen to the comfortable sitting room. Hunter sat down by her on the sofa where he'd fallen asleep what now seemed like ages ago. Robicheaux sat in a club chair opposite them.

"So, what is this major development?" Robicheaux asked.

"To start with, you were right when you said Elizabeth's killer was a copycat and not the same man who'd killed the first three victims."

"Always good to be right," Robicheaux said. "Is that a sure thing or a theory?"

"As of about two hours ago, we have confirmed DNA evidence to back it up."

Helena listened as Hunter explained how a man named Eric Presserman who was recently released from prison saw information about the reward money that Mia helped raise and came forward to tell what he knew.

"He claimed that while he was serving time at Angola, one of his cell mates, Samson Everson, who was in on armed robbery, bragged to him about killing two young women in swamps near New Orleans and throwing their bodies to the alligators.

"Samson didn't just tell him the basics, he provided all the gory details. Told him how he tied the victims' panties to tree branches and the bizarre pattern of slash marks left on their breasts. Information that was never released to the public, so Presserman would have had to get it from the killer."

"Crazy that when a man gets away with murder, he can't keep his mouth shut," Robicheaux said. "What else did the fool brag about?"

"He said he still dreamed of killing beautiful young women and couldn't wait to get out of prison and do it again. He already had his next victim picked out."

"Where is Everson now?" Robicheaux asked.

"Dead. What was left of his body was found in his torched and totaled car a few days before the third murder. No one tied him to the murder of the earlier two women."

"And they didn't check the DNA at the time?" Helena asked.

"They should have," Hunter agreed. "If they did, the results were never flagged and have since disappeared from the system."

"That sounds a bit suspicious," Helena said.

"Screwups happen sometimes," Hunter said.

"Son of a bitch," Robicheaux said. "A greedy ex-con spits out more information in one day than the task force has collected in almost six months. Guess I'm losing my touch."

"Thank goodness that sooner or later most criminals make mistakes," Hunter said, "like not being able to refrain from bragging about what they got away with."

Helena turned to Hunter. "But you still don't know who killed the third victim and then Elizabeth—or why. Or who is calling me on the phone claiming to be the killer. Now I wonder if that's even related to Elizabeth's murder. The caller might be some fruitcake trying to get in on the act, too. Another copycat. Perhaps he's not even dangerous. Except the killer talked about Elizabeth's red panties in one of his calls to Mia."

"Right. We still have every reason to believe your caller killed Elizabeth and likely the third victim, too."

"Once you kill someone and watch them die, it can get in your blood," Robicheaux said. "That's one thing I learned while working at the FBI."

Helena cringed.

"Not always," Hunter said, "but too often."

"The new developments provide the chief of police and the mayor something to dangle in front of the citizens as a sign of progress, but it doesn't lower the danger risk," Robicheaux said.

Hunter laid a hand on Helena's. "The good news is that you no longer have to worry about talking to the suspect. His calls will go straight to my phone and to the police tracking device."

"No," Helena said, without hesitation. "The caller thinks he has some connection to me. Even if you're not able to locate and arrest him via the call, he may slip and confess something to me just like Samson Everson did to his cell mate."

"It's not worth the risk," Hunter insisted.

"It will be if it stops a murder."

"Helena's right," Robicheaux said. "Once this new information hits the airwaves, things will change. If he gets nervous enough, he may give her something—anything—to help us identify and arrest him."

"Helena's not bait," Hunter said.

"I am if that's what it takes," Helena said. "Besides, I have complete trust that you'll protect me."

Complete trust. The one thing people kept warning her not to have.

"I like the way you think, Helena," Robicheaux said. "And once I get the new security system up and fully operating, I can guarantee you that no one will come into this house unless you let them in."

Helena wrapped her arms about her chest. "Which is close to what Elizabeth did when she went with her killer willingly."

Robicheaux rubbed the back of his neck as if his muscles were too tight. "There's no one hundred percent way to know that's exactly how that went down."

"True," Hunter agreed. "Everything we were sure of before is now suspect in my mind since we found out we're dealing with a copycat killer."

"I think it's someone close to home—too close," Helena said. "Possibly someone Ella sees as a friend. But then he must have been someone who'd heard Samson Everson's story, too."

"If Everson talked to Presserman, there's a good chance he talked to others," Robicheaux said.

Hunter and Robicheaux talked for another ten minutes, but Helena stopped trying to follow the conversation when the police jargon started to flow. She kept thinking of Elizabeth who'd been killed by a crazed copycat who treated life and death like a game.

Brigitte's warning echoed through her mind. She doubted either of the men would put much stock in the words of an elderly psychic in a senior living center, yet Helena couldn't ignore Brigitte's alarm.

She turned to face Hunter. "I never got a chance to tell you what Brigitte Orillon said when Alyssa and I were leaving the assisted living center where she lives today."

"Brigitte Orillon?" Robicheaux repeated. "Isn't that the psychic who used to claim she could solve crimes?"

"Supposedly she used to be a medium," Helena said.

Robicheaux frowned. "If she's the same one I've heard of, she must be a hundred years old by know."

"Not quite." Helena left it at that.

"What did Brigitte say?" Hunter asked.

"That the killer is coming after me but that there will be two victims."

"Don't let her frighten you with that ballyhoo," Robicheaux said.

"I'm just repeating her words."

Hunter took Helena's hand and squeezed it. "I'm doing my best to see that there are *no* victims. And even if there are, no matter what the Orillons conjure up, you are not going to be one of them."

Robicheaux nodded. "And I'll be right there to see that Hunter has all the help he needs even if it means me moving in with you to be here when Hunter can't."

"I trust you with her life, but not anywhere near her bed," Hunter quipped.

Helena wasn't sure he was joking.

Hunter stood. "I hate to leave such good company,

but I've got to go now. If I'm late, I'll catch hell from the chief."

Helena walked Hunter to the door. He held her in his arms and the thrill of being near him rocked her to her soul. Still she couldn't help thinking about Brigitte's words. Two victims.

"Does Lacy have full-time police protection?" Helena asked.

"She will now, as a precaution until she leaves the area. But she won't be aware of it."

"Thanks. That eases my mind. Will you be back tonight?" she asked, trying not to sound needy or afraid.

"I'll be back if you want me."

"I do."

"I'm not sure when. Barker and I will probably be working into the wee hours of the morning with all the new information we have to check out."

"I can go to the store and pick up something for dinner," Helena offered. "It's finally cool enough we could eat on the balcony by candlelight."

"How am I supposed to resist an invitation like that?"

"I was being quite selfish and hoping you couldn't."

"Barker won't like it, but I can probably get away for an hour or so around eight. You light the candles. I'll bring wine and dinner from my favorite steak house."

He trailed kisses from her earlobe to her lips.

And then he was gone, leaving her hungry for more of him.

Robicheaux took his time, hanging around until the

press conference started. She had no choice but to invite him to watch it with her in the sitting room.

She would have preferred watching it without his commentary so that she could fully appreciate how intelligent, professional and gorgeous Hunter looked giving his spiel.

When the press conference was over, she practically pushed Robicheaux out the door. She went upstairs and was just stepping out of her clothes to shower when her phone rang.

She grabbed the phone and checked the caller ID. Randi. Terrible timing, but it could be important.

"I've got great news for you," Randi said as soon as they got past the hellos.

That, Helena wasn't expecting. "What kind of news?"

"I think we have a buyer and from what I hear, he's willing to pay the full appraisal price and possibly more."

Helena swallowed hard. A promising, prospective buyer. That's what she'd come back to New Orleans for. She should be jubilant. Instead anxiety settled like lead weights in her chest.

"Who is the interested party?" she asked.

"I'm not sure. I'm talking to the man's Realtor agent at this point, but it sounds like we're dealing with a celebrity of some sort or perhaps foreign royalty. He doesn't want his name revealed and he doesn't plan to use it for rental property so either he has a huge family or expects a lot of visitors."

Last Tuesday Helena would have been thrilled with

this offer. That was before she'd reunited with Hunter, before he'd turned her world upside down. Before they'd made love.

She better understood his reasons for leaving before, but his miserable past was still his past. Could he promise and deliver forever, or would he walk away and break her heart again?

If he did, how would she ever get over that?

"I can request an appraisal tomorrow," Randi said. "Get that and then we'll see how serious our mystery buyer is."

Helena couldn't say yes—or no. "I need time to think this over."

"I don't recommend waiting around long," Randi said. "Real estate offers can go from hot to icy cold fast. Getting an appraisal doesn't obligate you to sell."

"You're right. I suppose an appraisal couldn't hurt."

"Agreed. I'll order one tomorrow and ask for a rush. I'm surprised you don't sound more excited, though. Are you having second thoughts about selling your late grandmother's beautiful home?"

Second thoughts. Third thoughts. All of them wrapped up in Hunter. "Perhaps," Helena admitted. "Let me know when you get the appraisal."

"Will do."

What she wanted was a lifetime of loving Hunter Bergeron. But it had to be all or nothing. No walking out when the going got tough. No crushing her heart and all her dreams again.

She needed commitment.

Chapter Fifteen

Hunter's spirits were plunging fast. With time of the essence, he and the rest of the task force seemed to be running in circles.

He pushed back from the table and walked over to their map of where each previous murder had taken place. "The first two victims no longer matter in the immediate scheme since their killer is dead. Presserman couldn't be the copycat killer since he was in prison during the third and fourth murders."

"The way I see it is our web grows smaller," Lane Crosby said. "I think we should narrow this down to a killer who knew Elizabeth and probably knew Mia Cosworth and possibly Helena, as well, before trying to figure out anyone's connection to Samson Everson or Presserman."

"So now we're looking for the man who killed victims three and four and then started making bizarre phone calls to first Mia and now Helena Cosworth," Barker said.

"And he's playing us like a well-tuned Stradivarius," Hunter said.

"Top of suspects on my list has always been Pierre Benoit," Barker said. "The guy's the perfect suspect and not just because I don't like his attitude. He speaks fluent French."

"He knew Mia, Ella and Elizabeth fairly well," Hunter said. "Plus, he's good-looking and suave enough that young women would be attracted to him."

"And he has an airtight alibi," Crosby reminded them.

"Or maybe not," Hunter said. "He was out of the country for the first two murders but not for Elizabeth's. Barker, how about you recheck which continent he was on at the time of the third murder?"

"How about we also put a tail on him for the next couple of days?" Barker said. "If he's Elizabeth's killer, he may lose his cool and try to skip town now that this new evidence is out."

"What about Connor Harrington?" Andy George asked. "I say we take another look at him, too."

"No reason not to." Hunter checked his watch. Eight o'clock. He expected an argument when he suggested they break for dinner. He didn't get it. Everyone was weary and hungry and needed some time with their family, but no one was ready to call it a night.

All five of the task force members agreed to meet back at ten to pore over the files for something they might have missed when they thought they were dealing with a serial killer who'd killed all four women.

Hunter called in a to-go order for filet mignons and salad from his favorite steak house. He'd make a quick stop at the liquor store, splurge for a bottle of good red wine and then he'd head straight for Helena's.

For the first time since he was a kid cowering from a drunken father, he was afraid. Afraid that he wasn't doing enough to protect Helena, though he had her house watched 24/7 and had her followed wherever she went.

But the brazen copycat killer was both incredibly evil and cunning. Hunter should never have let Helena take the phone calls from a maniac. He should have encouraged her from the first to go back to wherever home was until the killer was arrested.

It wasn't too late. Getting out of that house and out of New Orleans was surely the safest course of action. She wasn't one to take orders, but he'd do his best to persuade her to leave right away.

Her safety was all that mattered.

THE CRESCENT MOON floated in the night sky surrounded by brilliant stars that put Helena's fluttering candle to shame.

She sat across the iron bistro table from Hunter sipping her wine on what should have been one of the most poignantly romantic moments of her life. Instead anxiety and tension flooded the space between them.

Her perfectly grilled filet was barely touched. Hunter's plate was clean, amazing considering the deep worry lines that furrowed his brow.

His kiss when he'd arrived had been both tender and strained. Conversation since then had been almost non-existent. But unspoken or not, the tension dominated the night and let heartbreaking memories sneak into her consciousness.

It was stress and fear brought on by his job that had ripped them apart before. That time the situation had hit too close to home for him. She understood that better after hearing about his tragic childhood, but still his drawing away now troubled her.

"Is there something you're not telling me?" she asked.

"I'm just thinking you must be wishing that you'd never come back to New Orleans even temporarily."

"I don't regret coming back, though I admit the timing is bad."

"Do you still have a house in the Boston area?" Hunter asked.

"Yes. And a new job starting in November."

"The job of your dreams. The life of your dreams."

"Who told you that?"

"Mia." He turned to face her, then reached across the table and took both her hands in his. "I've given this a lot of thought, Helena. I think you should take the first flight back to Boston either tonight or in the morning."

She swallowed hard. "Are you that eager to get rid of me?"

"I'm that determined to keep you safe until the killer is off the streets. Hopefully that will be soon. Don't tell anyone you know around here where you are going. No one, not even Ella."

"Ella's not a killer."

"No, but she's a talker."

"Then you think the killer is someone she's close to?" Helena asked.

"I've never ruled that out."

Helena's resolve swelled. "I appreciate your concern, but I'm not going anywhere, Hunter. I'm the only personal contact you have with the French Kiss Killer. One more phone call might give us that breakthrough moment."

"I've gone along with you until now," Hunter said, "but the game has become too deadly. Even in Boston, you'll need a bodyguard. Robicheaux can hook you up with one."

"I'm not going anywhere. You do your job—I'll be here waiting for the bastard's call."

Hunter pushed back from the table. "There's a law against ignoring a policeman's orders."

"Really? Then arrest me."

"I'm considering that. Until I do, I'm moving Doug Conn into the carriage house with you tonight. He's not a member of the task force but he's one of the best detectives in the department. No one will get by him."

"If that's what it takes, then bring him on."

HELENA WAS EVEN more stubborn than Hunter remembered. It was an exasperating trait and weirdly he loved her all the more for it. She'd always gone after what she wanted.

At one time that had been him. He'd blown that. Now it was apparently a career in Boston she needed. Somehow, he couldn't imagine himself fitting in her art world.

Mia had suspected that all along. She hadn't specifically pointed out that Helena's life was better without him in it. Her words had been more tactful, but the
message had been clear. Clearer yet had been her con-
viction that he'd broken Helena's heart once and that
she didn't deserve that from him again.

He agreed. He loved Helena too much to ever put
her through any kind of pain again. How could he ask
her to give up a life she loved, one that challenged her
great talent, to be with him?

And how in the world could he ever give her up
again?

His phone vibrated, and he took a call from Barker.

"What's up?"

"I told you I wanted to put a tail on Pierre Benoit."

"Yeah. Did the chief balk on that?"

"No, but so far we haven't been able to locate him.
A neighbor said she saw him leaving with a suitcase a
couple of hours ago. I managed to get in touch with his
supervising attorney at the law firm where he works.
He said Pierre came in right before he left work today
and requested a week's emergency leave."

"Did he get it?"

"He did. If I can't locate Pierre soon I'll put out an
APB as a person of interest."

Robicheaux and Barker had considered Pierre Benoit
a serious suspect from the beginning. Maybe he should
have paid more attention to their hunches all along.

The clanging of garbage cans and the odor of fresh
brewed coffee woke Helena from a restless sleep. She

rolled over and experienced a sinking feeling when she realized that Hunter wasn't in bed with her. Evidently Doug Conn had brewed the coffee.

The grandfather clock on the landing chimed six times as she stretched and kicked off the top sheet. The air-conditioning was already cranking away even though thunderstorms and a dip in the temperature were forecast for late afternoon.

There had been no call from the killer that night. Weirdly, she regretted that, even though a madman's call in that spine-tingling child's voice tore her apart. But at least a call from him offered one more chance to locate him before it was too late.

Hunter had stayed until Doug Conn arrived for duty last night. Helena had hated to see him leave, but Doug had proved to be super nice and very professional.

He'd set up his laptop on the seldom used dining room table and assured her he was armed and ready to protect. She'd only seen the pistol he wore at his waist but suspected he had another weapon or two on him somewhere.

She slid her feet into her slippers, stepped over to the sliding glass door and opened the lightweight privacy drapes. The gloomy gray of predawn was depressing.

The two chairs pushed away from the table were bitter reminders of how quickly last night's dinner had gone from promising to a clash of wills. But the evening had still ended with a kiss at the door.

She walked to the bathroom, splashed her face with cold water and tamed her hair with a few strokes from her hairbrush.

She slipped into a full-skirted cotton dress and a pair of sandals and started down the staircase toward the inviting odor of coffee.

It was still impossible to descend the stairs without thinking of her grandmother and how much she missed her. She didn't doubt that Mia had discouraged Hunter from looking her up when he'd moved back to New Orleans.

She knew better than anyone how long it had taken for Helena to get her life back on track after their breakup. Nonetheless, the final decision not to contact Helena had still been Hunter's.

That was all in the past. The issues now were more confusing. Was the magic she felt with him lasting, or was it the danger that intensified their emotions to a fever point? Did he want her to leave because he thought their relationship was moving too fast, or was it purely for her own safety?

"Hope I didn't wake you," Doug said as she joined him in the kitchen.

"No, I'm an early riser—even when my life is normal. Have you heard from Hunter?"

"A couple of times during the wee hours of the morning and again about thirty minutes ago," Doug said.

So Hunter had no doubt had little or no sleep last night. "Are there any new developments in the case?"

"A couple, but I'll let him tell you about them. He asked that you call when you woke. He didn't want to disturb you. Coffee's fresh if you want some."

"Thanks." She poured herself a cup. "I can cook

you some bacon and pancakes after I talk to Hunter or there's my standby of yogurt and granola that you can help yourself to."

"Actually, I'll be leaving as soon as my replacement gets here. Hunter will fill you in on that."

"Then if you'll excuse me, I'll take my coffee onto the private courtyard patio and call Hunter."

"Is that the one off the downstairs bedroom?"

"Yes."

"I'll walk out with you and secure the area and then give you all the privacy you need."

In many ways this level of protection was more frightening than being on her own, a constant reminder that she was living under a time bomb of danger.

But if Brigitte had been right, there would be two victims. Was there some young woman right now going about her life with no hint that someone was stalking her and planning her murder?

Five minutes later, Helena had settled in a dark green Adirondack chair with a view of the privacy fence that surrounded her, pots of late-blooming asters and lantana and a male cardinal who perched on the top of a standing bird feeder. Hunter's phone rang twice before he answered.

"Doug said you wanted me to call."

"Yeah. I did. Can I call you right back, ten minutes or less?"

"Certainly."

He sounded weary and a little edgy. Hopefully it was not because the killer had struck during the night. She finished her coffee and set the empty cup on the table beside her chair, scaring off a gecko who tumbled to the stone floor.

She grabbed the phone when it rang. "Hello."

"Sorry about that, but I was on the phone with Barker and it couldn't wait."

"A new development?" she asked, praying it was a good one.

"Pierre Benoit was picked up for questioning in Dallas, Texas, a couple of hours ago."

"Pierre? Questioned about what? You surely don't think he killed Elizabeth."

"That hasn't been ruled out completely, but apparently his sudden departure from his home and job here is a result of his mother having a stroke yesterday."

"Oh, dear. I'm sorry to hear that."

"We all are. He was released immediately."

"Anything else happen while I slept?"

"Several more leads phoned in after the publicity yesterday. We're checked them out, but so far nothing is jelling."

"I was almost sure the killer would call last night," Helena said, thinking out loud. "He seems to enjoy the game of cat and mouse so much."

"About last night," Hunter said. "I know I came on strong, but you have to understand that it's not some unreasonable cop machoism. It's that I can't do my job here unless I know I'm doing everything possible to protect you."

"I know that and I appreciate it."

"Did things work out okay with Doug?"

"Perfect. He's super professional."

"One of the most trusted guys on the force in my mind. So is his replacement today. Ralph Bellinger. You'll like him."

"Do you really think it's necessary I have someone in the house with me during the daylight?"

"Humor me."

"I will. You outrank me. Just one more quick question. Do you know how much longer Lacy and her friend will be in New Orleans?"

"They are flying home tomorrow afternoon."

"That makes me feel better. Will I see you again today?"

"I was afraid you might not want me to after last night."

"I very much want to. Please take care of yourself, Hunter." She wanted to say more, like I love you. The timing seemed all wrong.

"See you the first chance I get. Until then Ralph will look after you, but I want you to seriously consider leaving town."

And though she hated to admit it, right now she did desperately miss her safe, peaceful life in Boston.

RALPH BELLINGER WAS as professional as Doug, staying out of Helena's way and leaving her to wander the carriage house as the hours dragged by. She tried cleaning out her grandmother's bedroom closet, but each item she touched brought her spirits even lower.

Thankfully, Ella walked over at noon and joined Helena for a sandwich and a glass of iced tea. Ella avoided talk about the new findings in Elizabeth's murder investigation in spite of the fact that it was all over the news.

Instead she relied on talk of the weather. Thunder rumbled in the distance and layers of dark clouds were rolling in.

"I know it sounds strange," Helena said, "but I've always liked thunderstorms. Not hurricanes or tornadoes, mind you, just the ferocity of an average New Orleans thunderstorm. They seem to wash away the staleness and revive the earth."

"It stormed the night Elizabeth was abducted."

"I didn't know that," Helena said.

"No reason you should."

There was no rage in Ella's voice. It was a statement of resignation, acknowledgement of a grief that would never be washed away.

Ella pushed away her half-eaten sandwich and wiped her mouth on the cloth napkin.

"It wasn't raining when Elizabeth left the house," Ella continued. "The sudden squall from the Gulf blew in around ten. I worried that she was cold and wet, never knowing that she was in the hands of a monster."

"I'm sorry." The expression was pathetically inadequate, but Helena couldn't think of anything that would ease Ella's pain.

"Your grandmother stood by me through it all. I don't think I would have survived without her."

"I know Mia was glad she could be here for you."

"She was amazing. She was always claiming she was close to identifying Elizabeth's killer. Bless her heart, I think she really believed that."

"But you didn't?"

"No. She sat around and read those books about serial killers until all hours of the morning. They put weird thoughts in her head. In the beginning, she'd actually suggested Hunter might be the killer because she figured he was mentally unstable when he called off your wedding. Then she got to know him and realized how smart and dedicated he really is."

Thunder rolled in the distance and the first streak of lightning split the clouds.

"I better get home before the monsoon hits," Ella said. She carried her plate and tea glass to the sink.

Helena walked her to the door and gave her a warm hug. "Call if you need anything," Helena said.

"I will. I know this is none of my business, but I don't think you should sell this house or the property. You belong here. You belong with Hunter."

Helena couldn't argue that.

She considered delving into the books on Mia's nightstand again but decided against it. Instead she walked upstairs and turned on her laptop.

She typed in French Kiss Killer and watched as a choice of articles popped up. She surfed down to one written by Antoine Robicheaux.

"Living in the Head of a Serial Killer."

She scanned the article, hitting only the main points. It emphasized that to identify and apprehend a serial killer, one had to think like the killer. Understand how he sees his world.

She skipped to another article by Robicheaux. This

one described how he'd assisted in apprehending several serial killers in states across the country.

She could see why Hunter thought so highly of him. She just hoped he came through this time.

ALYSSA ORILLON CLOSED the door behind a customer and staggered to her chair, suddenly so dizzy and disoriented her feet couldn't find the floor.

She'd been fine earlier in the day when Lacy Blankenship and two of her friends had stopped in, but within minutes after they'd left, she'd developed a case of vertigo. She'd had to lie down for a half hour to regain her equilibrium.

That was over an hour ago. Now, she was developing a brain-crushing headache to go with her nausea.

And still she couldn't get Lacy Blankenship off her mind.

Lacy was the only one who'd wanted a psychic session. She was positively giddy as she'd described her obsession with an older man she'd met in New Orleans. She wanted Alyssa to offer assurances that this sophisticated charmer she'd fallen in love with at first sight loved her as much as she loved him.

Alyssa didn't have to be a medium to realize the vacation affair with an older pursuer wasn't likely the real thing. Even in Lacy's love-crazed description of him, he sounded like a player.

She'd delicately warned Lacy not to invest too much of herself into the relationship until she'd known the man longer. Separation wouldn't tear them apart if he was the right man for her. Alyssa seriously doubted her words had affected the impressionable young woman.

Now all Alyssa could think of was Lacy and her likeness to Elizabeth, who had also trusted the wrong man.

Alyssa put her head back and closed her eyes. Her head begin to spin and then the dark, bloody images from the other night struck like waves of neon lights crashing into her brain.

Only now it was Lacy and Helena on the run, sloshing through mud and standing water, the man with the knife chasing them through the fog.

The images zoomed in and out, faster and faster. Her stomach retched. She made it to the bathroom just in time to lose her lunch. Shaking and weak, she went back to the chair where she'd been sitting, picked up her phone and punched in Helena's number.

Chapter Sixteen

But occasionally a successful serial killer defied all odds, his skill coming from his superior intellect and his motivation via the thrill of power. That made him almost impossible to track down and apprehend.

HELENA'S PHONE RANG as she finished reading the disturbing words from one of her grandmother's collection of articles.

"Hello."

"Helena. It's Alyssa." Her voice was so shaky Helena could barely understand her.

"What's wrong?"

"I need to talk to you. Can I come over now?"

"No. You sound ill. I'll call 911."

"No. It's the images again, the ones from the other night. I'm so afraid for you. I think the killer is about to strike."

Alyssa was clearly shaken. Her fear was real. Her facts were sketchy. "Stay put. I'll be there as fast as I can."

"You can't come alone. It's too dangerous."

"Rest assured. There's no chance of my doing this solo. My bodyguard won't allow it."

She broke the connection and stepped onto her balcony. The air was still muggy, but dark clouds had rolled in. A lightning bolt streaked across the sky followed by a deafening clap of thunder. The full force of the storm would hit any minute.

Helena grabbed an umbrella and raced down the stairs. Ralph heard her approach and was waiting for her at the foot of the staircase.

"Whoa there. Where do you think you're rushing off to with that umbrella?"

"My friend Alyssa Orillon just called. She's hallucinating about the serial killer and is practically hysterical. I have to calm her down."

"I have strict orders from Hunter that you're not to leave the house. If you try, I have to contact him."

"You do what you need to. I'm doing what I have to."

Helena had no doubt that Ralph would follow her or that he'd contact Hunter who'd have someone follow her.

Ralph's footsteps sounded behind her, keeping up with her fast pace even though she could hear him talking on his phone. She unlocked the gate, shoved it open and took off at a jog.

An elderly couple had stopped on the sidewalk and were struggling to open a stubborn umbrella in preparation for the deluge that would hit soon. Any other time Helena would have stopped to help and encouraged them to seek shelter before the inevitable torrents of rain arrived.

Another lightning and thunder duo hit as she reached the corner. The sidewalks were mostly empty now, though a group of millennials, likely tourists, were dancing around across the street from her and sipping daiquiris from red to-go cups as if the storm was reason to party.

Helena glanced around. Ralph was a mere step behind her. If anyone had noticed them, they might have thought he was chasing her. She was two blocks from Alyssa's when the first fat drops of rain pelted the top of her head and her face.

A gust of cold wind whipped her hair into her eyes and sent the rain flying at her sideways, prickling her skin like needles. She slowed enough to open her umbrella before crossing the street in the middle of the block to reach the side with more store awnings for protection.

As she stepped onto the curb, an even stronger gust of wind hit, reversing her umbrella and almost blowing it from her hands. Trying to control it threw her off balance. She tripped, and her feet went flying from beneath her.

Two strong arms wrapped around her a second before her butt hit the sloshing water. She turned around, expecting her rescuer to be Ralph. It wasn't.

"Hunter. How did you get here at that exact moment?"

"I'm like Superman. I sense when a lovely damsel is in distress."

"More like a half-drowned, clumsy damsel."

"I never said I was picky."

He led her to a storefront of a souvenir shop and they huddled close to the glass, protected by the large awning. Her damp hair dripped down her face and tickled her eyelashes. His arm was around her shoulders.

Her gaze met Hunter's. His fingers trailed a path down her wet cheeks until he slid his thumb beneath her chin and nudged her mouth to his. His lips found hers and she melted into his sweet, poignant kiss. In the midst of a storm, her life in danger from a madman, she had never felt so protected or loved.

The rain continued to fall in deluges for several minutes, finally slowing to a shower as the ferocity of the storm gave way to the first cool front of autumn.

"Tell me what's up with Alyssa," he said, his deep voice more gravelly than it had been before their kiss.

"She's seeing those visions again and they have thrown her into a state of hysteria."

"I thought you told me she doesn't claim to have any clairvoyant powers."

"That's what she says, but still she's unable to dismiss the images as being irrelevant."

"Then I guess we better go check her out."

"You don't have to go with me," she said. "I know how busy you are. I didn't tell Ralph to call you."

"I'm busy looking for a killer who's playing me for a fool. I've spent hours upon hours chasing rabbits. What can I lose by spending a few minutes with a psychic?" He ran his hand across her shoulder blades and let his fingers tangle in her hair. "Besides, I'm not about to turn down a legitimate reason for spending some time with you."

"I like that." She turned around suddenly realizing her previous bodyguard was nowhere in sight. "Where's Ralph?" she asked as Hunter raised his umbrella.

"Taking a break before going back to the carriage house. I told him when I caught up with him that you're in my hands for now."

"Very good hands," she agreed as they started sloshing through and around puddles toward Alyssa's.

HUNTER HAD TO admit that talking to psychics made him uncomfortable. He figured to each his own when it came to making a living as long as it didn't hurt anyone else, but he couldn't buy into the sixth sense business.

Nonetheless, the minute they walked in her door, he could see that she was shaken. He listened and let Helena do the talking at first but joined in the conversation when they got down to the direct facts of the matter.

"It started as soon as Lacy and her friends left," Alyssa explained. "Well, actually, I was uncomfortable talking to Lacy about this man she'd met while here on vacation. It got worse from there."

"Who were the friends that were with her?" Hunter asked.

"Her friend Brenda who was with her when she came originally, though I didn't know her name on that first visit. And a slightly older woman named Courtney."

If Courtney was with them, there was much less to worry about. "Tell me again what Lacy said about this man and try to leave nothing out."

The story Alyssa told about falling for a gorgeous stranger could probably describe hundreds of tourists a year. "Did Lacy tell you his name?"

"No. I asked, but she said she'd rather keep that a secret. That's not why I think she's in danger," Alyssa insisted. "It's the phantasms that haunt me."

"Phantasms? Not sure I know what those are," Hunter admitted.

"Ghostlike creatures. Only they weren't ghosts, they were bloody images of real people. Lacy and Helena and a man who's always too blurry to recognize."

"I know the idea of a serial killer right here in the French Quarter is frightening," Hunter said. "But remember that we have zero evidence that the serial killer has ever seen Lacy, much less that she's his target."

"But Lacy looks so much like Elizabeth," Alyssa argued. "If he merely ran into her on the streets, he'd have to see that. Whatever attracted him to Elizabeth would attract him to Lacy, too."

"That's possible, which is why I'll check on Lacy. Is there somewhere private I can make a phone call?"

"Yes, in my studio." She crossed the room and opened the door for him. One step inside and he felt like he'd entered the inner realm of some magical Greek goddess.

A bowl of fragrant vapors, dim lighting, a glowing crystal ball, a set of cards spread out on the silk-covered table. And creepy background music that he'd only heard before in haunted houses at Halloween.

He made a call to Courtney to verify that Lacy was safe.

She answered on the first ring.

"Thanks for calling me back so soon, Hunter."

"If you called me earlier, I didn't get the message. I was just calling you to make sure everything is going okay."

"I just left the message at the precinct. We have a problem."

Not what he wanted to hear.

"Lacy has disappeared."

"Do you have any idea where she is or who she's with?"

"I do."

His insides took a hit as he listened to the details. He prayed his worst fears were all wrong and wished to God he didn't have to tell this to Helena. But she deserved the truth. There wasn't enough sugar in the world to fully coat this but he'd damn sure try.

Chapter Seventeen

Hunter didn't give any verbal indication the news was bad when he rejoined Helena and Alyssa, but Helena knew that was the verdict from the extended veins in his neck and his strained facial expression.

He tried to reassure Alyssa that things were under control. He was good at that and she did seem to be feeling a little better when they left.

Helena waited until they were out the door before she confronted Hunter. "What's the real story?"

He reached down, took her hand and squeezed it. "Nothing you want to hear."

"I know you only want to protect me, Hunter, but I don't want to be protected from the truth. Did you talk to Courtney or just to one of the other officers involved in the investigation?"

"I talked to Courtney."

"Is she still with Lacy and Brenda?"

"She's with Brenda. Lacy seems to have disappeared."

"Disappeared from where? The hotel?"

"The city."

Panic painted ugly pictures in her mind. She struggled to stay reasonably calm.

"The three of them were having lunch and a beer at the Crescent City Brewhouse. They were almost through eating when Lacy excused herself to go the restroom and didn't return."

"So she just walked out on them. Did they have an argument?"

"According to Courtney, everything seemed to be going great except that Lacy was even livelier and more animated than usual."

None of this made sense. Surely no one abducted her in the middle of the day. "When did this happen?"

"Approximately a half hour ago. They started to worry after about ten minutes. They searched the bathroom and outside the building. There was no sign of her. The rain had started by then so it was very unlikely she stepped outside to make a phone call or write a text."

"Did they try to text her?"

"They called her and then they answered her phone. She'd left it on the table with them so they couldn't possibly reach her."

"Did they see her talking to anyone who looked suspicious either inside or outside the restaurant?"

He shook his head. "Don't jump to the worst conclusions, Helena."

"You mean like the fact that the French Kiss Killer told me it was full speed ahead or that Lacy looks enough like the last young woman he'd murdered that they could be twins?"

"Or more likely, she's slipped off to see her new love interest that she told Alyssa about."

"Do they know who that is?"

"Brenda has strong suspicions. She thinks Lacy has been sneaking out to meet Connor Harrington after he goes off duty at night."

"Connor, my engaged tenant? What a jerk. Lacy is years too young…"

She stopped midsentence as a terrifying possibility rushed her brain. "Oh my God. Surely he didn't kill Elizabeth. He's not planning to kill Lacy."

"More likely he's a jerk who two-times his fiancée, but I'm heading over to the Aquarelle Hotel now to question him about his relationship to Lacy and see if they're up to a little afternoon delight or if he knows where she is."

"And if he's not there?" she asked, her fears multiplying even with no real evidence.

"If he's not there, we'll find him. I had hoped we could grab a quick lunch before I had to jump back into the fray but looks like that's out of the question. I'll walk you home. It's barely out of the way."

"I'll save you the trouble," Helena said, the plan forming in her mind as she spoke. "I'm going to the hotel with you."

"This is police business. I can't take a civilian into that situation."

"Then I'm going without you. As a friend of Lacy, I have every right to talk to him myself."

"You're not a friend of Lacy's."

"Close enough." She started walking.

Hunter tried to grab her wrist. She shoved him away and kept walking.

"At least let me do all the talking," Hunter ordered.

She made no promises.

Fifteen minutes later Helena and Hunter were seated in Connor's office, sipping hot coffee from deep blue mugs that had been brought in by one of his waitresses. Connor sat across from them, tapping nervously on the table.

"This isn't the best time for me to chat," Connor said, "but since you insisted we meet, I assume this is police business."

"It is," Hunter said.

Connor nodded toward Helena. "So why is she here?"

"She's concerned about a young woman who's a guest in your hotel."

"It's not my job to keep up with the guests. It's my job to make sure they're comfortable and satisfied."

"Have you been satisfying Lacy Blankenship this afternoon?" Helena asked, letting the reproachful words slip out before she could stop them.

Hunter glared at her.

Connor ignored her question and kept facing Hunter. "What is this about? Are you accusing me of something?"

"No," Hunter answered. "We're just trying to track down Miss Blankenship. It seems she's lost her phone and no one can reach her."

"Have you contacted her friend Brenda who's traveling with her? You can usually find the two of them together."

"Not this time. Brenda is the one who brought her sudden disappearance to our attention."

"I'm sorry, but I can't help you with that."

"Brenda seems to think you've been hanging out with Lacy after closing time," Hunter said.

"Is that against the law these days?"

"No," Hunter said.

"Regardless, I haven't seen her after work or any other time except to speak to her inside the hotel common areas. I'm engaged to be married to a beautiful and wonderful woman. I love her and there is no way I'm going to mess up what we have with a fling. Besides, it would be against company policy and I'm not doing anything to blow this job."

Helena had to admit he sounded sincere, and she wanted to believe him. She'd always liked Connor. But the anxiety burning in her chest wouldn't quit.

"Do you have security cameras in the hallway?" Helena asked.

"Antoine Robicheaux's company installed all of our security features," Connor assured her. "They're the best in the business. I'd need a warrant to release private information on my guests."

"No warrant at this point," Hunter said. "I would like to check her room to make sure she hasn't injured herself and can't call for help."

"Good idea," Connor agreed willingly. "I'll check her room number and walk you up there."

In case she'd been injured or met with foul play. Helena knew exactly what he really meant.

"You'll need to wait here, Miss Cosworth," Connor said. "Company policy when I open someone's room for the police."

"No problem."

Apprehension ran ragged races along her nerves until they returned ten minutes later. The room search had revealed nothing. Suitcases and clothes were still in the closets and there was no sign of foul play.

"So, that's it?" Helena questioned as they left the hotel.

"I can't exactly arrest him due to rumors he may be having a consensual affair."

"But what if he knows where Lacy is? What if…"

Hunter interrupted her with a finger to her lips. "I'm a good cop, Helena, with great instincts. I think Connor was telling the truth."

"But if you're wrong?"

"Then we're still covered. I'll put a tail on him until Lacy shows up."

"I'm sorry," she said. "You're the detective. I'm not. But this is all so frightening and nerve-racking."

"I know. For all of us. I'm just trying to do my job the best I know how. I'll put my life on the line in a heartbeat to save an innocent life—the same way everyone on the investigative force will. But just so you know, keeping you safe is the most important thing in my life right now."

He pulled her into his arms and touched his lips to

hers. She trembled, not from fear, but from the intensity of the emotions coursing through her veins.

"Thanks for being a hero," she said when he let her go. "Thanks for looking after me."

"Always."

Always would be almost long enough for her.

THE RAIN HAD slowed to a mist when he spotted Lacy, waiting for him in the narrow alleyway where he'd told her to meet him. He scanned the area to make sure no one was watching and then stopped next to the dumpster.

He reached across the seat and opened the passenger side door. She smiled and climbed in.

"I was afraid you weren't coming," she said, leaning over for a kiss as he drove to the corner.

"I'm right on time," he said, just as he'd planned it. "Have you seen anyone since you got here?"

"No people. I was checked out by a calico cat and a couple of roaches large enough to give the curious cat a ride on their backs. This disgusting alley stinks."

"Sorry about that but it can't be helped."

"How long do we have to keep our feelings for each other a secret?"

"One more night, and then you can tell the world."

"You're so mysterious."

"That's what you love about me." He chuckled as he reached over and ran his right hand between her legs. This would be so easy. He turned right at the corner.

"Where are we going?" Lacy asked.

"To a hideaway in Algiers."

"A hotel?"

"Nothing that boring," he teased.

"I don't even know where Algiers is, but I can't wait."

"Only a short drive away, I promise. And then we'll have the whole night together."

"I'll need to use your phone to call Brenda before dark and let her know I'm safe."

"Of course, my sweet. We can do whatever you want." Tonight would be his grand finale, the end of his career as the French Kiss Killer.

Two more murders and then he'd have to let this dark side of him die with the murderous legend. Part of being a successful serial killer was knowing when to let the identity fade into oblivion. Even he couldn't outsmart everyone forever.

Tonight, he'd have the ultimate orgasm as he watched two beautiful women fighting for their last breaths before he tossed them overboard to the hungry gators who lived in the swampy waters.

And no one would ever guess that the killer had been in their midst all the time.

HELENA RECEIVED A phone call from Hunter at ten o'clock that evening. He gave her a quick update on the quickly emerging situation.

Lacy Blankenship had not been found. Her friend Brenda was an emotional train wreck and was talking to every reporter who'd listen to her. She'd also called Lacy's parents.

It was the first they'd heard of the French Kiss

Killer. They were desperate and had booked the first flight to New Orleans the following morning.

"I'd hoped I could get back there to at least tell you good night in person, but that looks impossible now."

"I understand. I'm in good hands with Cory Barker tonight, but what happened to Doug Conn? Did he have enough of me already?"

"He's taking the second shift tonight," Hunter said. "Rest assured, no way is anyone getting the best of Barker."

"I'm convinced," she said. "Don't worry about me. I'm more concerned about you."

"Don't be. I plan to still be alive to celebrate when the French Kiss Killer goes down. Tell Barker I'll get back to him later. Gotta run now, but…" He hesitated. "About the other night when I said you should go to Boston. That was only about keeping you safe. I hope you know that."

"Let's save the subject of Boston for another night."

They said their goodbyes and she walked back into the kitchen. Barker was spooning vanilla ice cream over a slice of apple pie Ella had brought over at dinnertime.

She filled him in on the latest news about Lacy. Neither of them mentioned that she might be in the hands of the serial killer, but the possibility silently overrode the conversation and the mood.

Barker wiped his mouth on a paper towel he'd taken from the counter. "You can tell me it's none of my business if you want, but what's the deal between you and Hunter? I know you used to date, but what broke you guys up? You seem to have a lot of chemistry going on between you now."

She started to evade a direct answer to Barker's question the way she usually did, but what was the point? It was fact.

"He left me at the altar."

"Hunter? Man, that doesn't sound like him."

"He had his reasons."

"That's a shocker. I figured it was the other way around. Your grandmother said you were a very talented artist with a promising career in Boston. Hunter doesn't seem like much of a fine arts connoisseur kind of guy so I figured you were too sophisticated for him."

"I am an artist and I do love everything about the art world and Boston, but that's not what broke us up."

"They have art in New Orleans—or so I've heard," Barker said. "I haven't actually seen any of it, well, except for the statues in the park and in St. Louis Cathedral. Any chance you'll move back here permanently and take over your grandmother's property?"

"There's always a chance." If she had something to come back for.

BY THE TIME Helena went to bed, the rain had stopped completely, and the clouds had thinned to the point where a few stars and a crescent moon found an occasional opening.

She'd left the curtains open, preferring a glimpse of moonlight to darkness tonight. Better to see the shadows creeping across her ceiling than to fight the nightmarish images flooding her subconscious.

It was past midnight the last time she'd checked the phone. The monster had still not called.

HELENA WAS WAKENED by the shrill ringing of her phone. Startled, she sat up in bed, heart pounding. The monster had finally called.

She reached for the wired phone but let her hand slide across it without picking it up when she realized it was her personal phone that was ringing. It must be Hunter calling with another update.

She stared out the sliding glass door and murmured hello in her sleep-heavy, husky voice.

"Bonjour, mademoiselle." Spoken in a soft, disguised voice.

Her heart jumped to her throat. The monster was always a step ahead.

"Who are you?" she begged. "Where are you?"

"Turn around and see."

Chapter Eighteen

Fear gripped Helena as she stood, turned and stared into the steel-gray eyes of Antoine Robicheaux. Only a few feet away. Smiling as if this were all a very sick joke.

"Not you. The monster can't be you."

Her pleadings of denial sounded brittle even to her own ears, as if fighting their way through a scream that was stuck in her throat.

"Don't be so surprised. No one is what they seem. Not even you. Given the right circumstances, every-one can kill."

"You're right. I could kill you right now and enjoy it."

But could she or would she hesitate even if the pistol Hunter had given her was in her hand?

"Did you kill Elizabeth Grayson?"

"No. That was the work of the French Kiss Killer." He smirked. "I'm part of the good guys team. Just ask Hunter."

"Do you have Lacy?"

"Are you jealous? Don't be. She's waiting on you in

the swamp. We should hurry. The gators will be getting hungry."

In one quick movement, she yanked open the drawer of her bedside table and went for the gun she'd never expected to fire. Before she could take aim, Robicheaux knocked the gun from her shaking grasp and slammed a fist into her stomach.

She doubled over in pain and finally the scream escaped. Shrill, loud, tearing from her throat like ripped tissue. There was no way Barker couldn't have heard her, but there was no response.

Robicheaux must have already killed him. She was on her own. She was no match for him physically, but if she could make it onto her balcony, some late-night partyers on the street might hear her scream.

But the bed was between her and the balcony and Robicheaux was between her and the stairs.

There was no exit. She had to fight. Still struggling to breathe after the punch in the stomach, she went for the bedside lamp.

Before she could tear the plug from the wall, he was on her again. She felt a sharp, piercing stab in her neck. She saw the needle as he pulled it from her flesh. She kicked and swung her fists, connecting only with air.

The room began to spin. Pinpricks of light went off inside her head like bottle rockets as Robicheaux bound her legs and wrists. She knew what he was doing, but she had no control of her body. No feeling of pain or movement.

Hunter would kill Robicheaux for this. Somehow,

he'd find out the truth and Robicheaux would pay. But it would be too late for Helena and Lacy.

I love you, Hunter. I haven't moved on. I couldn't. You never let go of my heart.

HELENA FADED IN and out of the comatose condition, unsure where she was even when she was partially alert, unable to scream or to speak, her body being bounced around as if she were on a carnival ride.

She had no idea how long she'd been floating in and out of consciousness. A moment? An hour? A day?

Finally, the movement stopped. She opened her eyes as metal clicked and could tell that she was lying in the trunk of a vehicle, a man staring down at her.

Romeo. Antoine Robicheaux. The monster. Confusion diffused enough that she remembered being abducted. She had no idea where he'd taken her. Her wrists and hands were bound in duct tape.

He lifted her roughly as if she were a sack of potatoes and then propped her against the back fender of a pickup truck. Her bare feet sank into a boggy quagmire.

He dragged her through an area that became continuously swampy as they went downhill toward a gray, weathered, ramshackle house like the ones Hunter had pointed out to her when they'd visited Eulalie.

But the area looked different. More trees with branches that canopied the dark water. A bayou that seemed to finger out in every direction.

She heard a splash and turned to watch an alligator

slide from the muddy bank and into a strand of slowly moving water.

When they reached the half-rotted steps to the front porch, Robicheaux picked her up, carried her inside and then dropped her onto a stained and dusty sofa.

Lacy was propped into a straight-backed chair a few feet away. Her wrists and feet were bound as well, and she was tied to the chair. A dirty rag had been stuffed into her mouth, no doubt to keep her from screaming while he had gone back for Helena.

Robicheaux walked over and yanked the rag from Lacy's mouth. "Scream and the party's over. You get me."

She nodded.

"You two enjoy your visit to the bayou. It's all part of the Louisiana adventure, Lacy. Helena can tell you all about it while I get your little surprise ready. I'll be back soon, but I want both of you to be fully alert for our next adventure. If you guessed it's a boat ride, you get the prize. We'll take the pirogue down the bayou and then we'll stop. I'll slice your breasts and your throats and watch while you choke to death on your gurgling blood. Then I'll toss you overboard."

Fury temporarily overrode Helena's fear. "You won't get away with this. Hunter will track you down. You'll see death from the other side and we'll see how brave you are then."

Lacy began to cry. "I thought you loved me. Why are you doing this?"

"Because I have no choice."

He stood silent for a long time and for the first time Helena thought she saw a trace of regret in his eyes.

"Why did you call my grandmother?" Helena asked the question that had burned in her mind ever since she'd arrived back in New Orleans.

"Because I liked her. If she hadn't fallen and died when she did, she might have been the one person who could have dragged me out of the darkness."

"It's not too late. You can walk away from this hell."

"I'll walk away when you two are dead."

He was truly mad.

Helena had to find a way to escape. Her wrists and ankles were still bound, but she could crawl and scoot across the floor. There must be something inside this house she could use as a weapon.

"Wait," Robicheaux said as he started to walk out the door. "I almost forgot, and it only takes one little mistake to take a killer down."

He walked back over and tied Helena's hands to a giant meat hook that hung from an iron overhead beam.

He was the devil himself.

"One more question," Helena said.

"Anything to make this good for you but make it quick."

"How did you know the man who had killed the first two women was dead before you killed the third woman and Elizabeth Grayson?"

"Because I'm an expert at what I do. I had tracked Samson Everson down. I was watching when he killed the second woman and I knew when he'd been released from prison and selected his third target. I killed him first."

The truth was sickening. "You could have saved the second victim, couldn't you? Instead you let her die and then you became the monster yourself. No wonder you know so much about how the brains of serial killers function. You are one."

"And now he's going to kill us." Tears rolled down Lacy's cheeks. "Please don't kill us," she begged. "I'll never tell anyone what you've done. Just let me live."

"It's too late for that now," Robicheaux said. "I have to see this through."

Helena waited until he was out of earshot before she tried to comfort Lacy. "Don't give up yet. As long as we're breathing, we have a chance. The smartest, bravest detective I know has promised to keep me safe. All we have to do is stay alive until he gets here."

She had no idea how he'd ever find them, but she had to hold on to something. She loved Hunter even more now than she had six years ago.

She had to live to tell him that.

Chapter Nineteen

Hunter was at a dead run when he reached the door to the carriage house. He'd tried to reach Barker and Helena on his way over. Neither had answered.

He couldn't imagine that anyone could have gotten past Cory Barker, but that didn't reduce the rising panic. He unlocked the door and rushed inside, Smith & Wesson in hand.

"Barker! Helena!" His frantic calls echoed through the house. The only response was a coughing noise as if someone was trying to clear their throat.

He followed the noise to the sitting room. He saw the blood splattered over the furniture and walls before he saw Barker. Barker was facedown in a pool of crimson.

Hunter fell to his knees and checked Barker's pulse. Almost too weak to be alive. He looked at the chest wound. The blood was starting to clot. "Where's Helena?" Hunter asked.

"He took her." Barker's voice was weak, the words whispered.

"Who took her? Who did this?"

"Romeo."

Curses flew from his mouth. "I'll kill him."

"Get on it."

"Do you know where they went?"

"Algiers. Swamp. First victim."

Fury and dread roared through Hunter as he called for an ambulance for Barker.

"Hold on. Help is coming, old buddy," Hunter said.

The French Kiss Killer had finally made a mistake. He'd thought Barker was struggling for his last breath when he couldn't resist bragging about his plan.

He should have known Barker was as tough as they came.

Hunter knew exactly where the first victim had been killed. He'd checked out the crime scene several times after the murder.

He didn't wait around for the ambulance. Barker needed a lot more help than he could give him.

He had to reach Helena in time.

TIME WAS RUNNING out for Helena and Lacy. Helena knew it, but still she cursed Robicheaux as he tucked her and Lacy into the hull of the long, narrow pirogue. With their wrists and ankles still bound, there was no way to roll into the water and try to swim to safety.

Their only chance of escape would be for Helena to get her hands on the hunting knife Robicheaux wore in a scabbard like a sword. Robicheaux stood in the back of the boat and poled them away from the muddy bank.

Their boat ride to hell had started.

Lacy screamed for help but there was no one to hear. Helena used her body to rock the boat, hoping

Robicheaux would fall on top of them and she could get her hands on that knife. It was a long shot. It was the only shot.

Robicheaux didn't fall. Instead, he dropped the pole inside the boat and unsheathed the knife. He raised it over her, ready to bury it in her chest or to slice her throat.

Her last thoughts were of Hunter and all the years they'd wasted.

Chapter Twenty

Hunter dodged branches, tangled vines and massive palmetto fronds as he raced toward the leaning, crumbling fishing cabin he remembered well. He'd parked uphill, above the worst of the swamp. He didn't want to be spotted until he was ready to spring into action.

The house was dark. Hunter's spirit plunged. He pushed himself to run faster, ignoring the pain in his chest and the cold, slimy snake he had to brush from his face after colliding with the branch of a cypress tree.

And then he heard the scream. Not coming from inside the house. He followed the sound, away from the house and toward the murky bayou.

He couldn't understand what had driven Robicheaux to this madness. It was of no concern now. All that mattered was stopping him before he killed Helena and probably Lacy, as well.

Hunter had lived through watching his father kill his mother. He didn't think he could live through losing Helena. Life couldn't take his world away again.

HELENA HELD HER breath as Robicheaux hesitated. He stared into the distance as if he'd heard or seen something that startled him.

She rocked the boat again. He fought to maintain his balance and then swung the knife at her face.

Gunfire cracked like fireworks. Robicheaux grabbed his chest with one hand and tried to bury the point of the knife inside her chest with the other. He missed by inches.

He collapsed and fell into the water, overturning the boat and dumping Helena and Lacy into the bayou. The whir of helicopters drowned out their cries for help.

Seconds later she and Lucy were surrounded by the most beautiful sight she'd ever seen. A NOPD rescue crew. Hunter was barking orders.

Someone pulled a deathly still Robicheaux from the water. A SWAT team member waded in to save Lacy. Hunter's arms encircled Helena as he pulled her to the bank.

Hunter cradled Helena in his arms, holding her as if he'd never let her go.

"I let you down," Hunter muttered. "I promised to protect you and I let you down."

"You saved my life. I kept telling myself you'd come but I don't think I believed it."

"I've never been that frightened before," he admitted. "I don't know how I could have gone on if I lost you."

"I love you, Hunter. I always have. I always will."

"Well, I guess that settles it then. Time for a move. What's the weather like in Boston this time of year?"

"Who needs Boston? Everything I've ever wanted is here."

Epilogue

Helena adjusted the skirt of the simple white wedding gown she'd purchased six years ago. She stepped into the courtyard on a beautiful, unusually warm December morning. She looked up and spotted Hunter standing beside the minister at the flower-bedecked altar.

He smiled. Her heart sang.

She walked past the rows of guests seated on folding chairs. She had no one to give her away. She needed no one. Mia's spirit accompanied her all the way.

Cory Barker sat with his wife and two daughters. Healing had been slow and painful, but he'd make a full recovery in time.

Ella had the seat of honor on the first row of folding chairs.

Alyssa was Helena's maid of honor.

Everything was perfect and yet Helena's hands grew clammy when the minister began the vows. Tears welled in her eyes as she whispered her "I do."

When it was Hunter's time to state his vows, the

love in his eyes convinced her that nothing would ever tear them apart again.

He said "I do" and the minister presented them as husband and wife.

"You may now kiss the bride."

Hunter did. The way all perfect weddings should end, as if a thousand brushstrokes had painted her world with love.

This time he was here to stay.

* * * * *

Get 4 FREE REWARDS!

We'll send you 2 FREE Books plus 2 FREE Mystery Gifts.

Harlequin Intrigue® books feature heroes and heroines that confront and survive danger while finding themselves irresistibly drawn to one another.

FREE Value Over **$20**

It's been years since Brock McGovern was last in his hometown—the place where he was once accused of a crime he did not commit. Now, with the help of his high school sweetheart, Maura Antrim, he's investigating another murder... But can they find a criminal who has always remained in the shadows?

Read on for a sneak preview of
Tangled Threat,
by New York Times *bestselling author Heather Graham.*

"I've been assigned to go back to Florida. To stay at the Frampton Ranch and Resort—and investigate what we believe to be three kidnappings and a murder. And the kidnappings may have nothing to do with the resort, nor may the murder?" Brock McGovern asked, a small note of incredulity slipping into his voice, which was surprising to him—he was always careful to keep an even tone.

FBI assistant director Richard Egan had brought him into his office, and Brock had known he was going on assignment—he just hadn't expected this.

"Yes, not what you'd want, but, hey, maybe it'll be good for you—and perhaps necessary now, when time is of the essence and there is no one out there who could know the place or the circumstances with the same scope and experience you have," Egan told him. "Three young women have disappeared from the area. Two of them were guests of the Frampton Ranch and Resort shortly before their disappearances—the third had left St. Augustine and was on her way there. The Florida Department of Law Enforcement has naturally been there already. They asked for federal help on this. Shades of the past haunt them—they don't want any more unsolved murders—and everyone is hoping against hope that Lily Sylvester, Amy Bonham and Lydia Merkel might be found."

"These are Florida missing-person cases," Brock said. "And it's sad but true that young people go to Florida and get caught up in the beach life and the club scene. And regrettable but true once again—there's a drug and alcohol culture that does exist and people get caught up in it. Not just in Florida, of course, but everywhere." He smiled grimly. "I go where I'm told, but I'm curious—how is this an FBI affair? And forgive me, but—FBI out of New York?"

"Not out of New York. FDLE asked for you. Specifically."

Don't miss
Tangled Threat *by Heather Graham,*
available September 2019 wherever
Harlequin® books and ebooks are sold.

www.Harlequin.com

HIEXP0819

Need an adrenaline rush from nail-biting tales
(and irresistible males)?

Check out **Harlequin Intrigue**®,
Harlequin® **Romantic Suspense** and
Love Inspired® **Suspense** books!

New books available every month!

CONNECT WITH US AT:

Facebook.com/groups/HarlequinConnection

Facebook.com/HarlequinBooks

Twitter.com/HarlequinBooks

Instagram.com/HarlequinBooks

Pinterest.com/HarlequinBooks

ReaderService.com

**ROMANCE WHEN
YOU NEED IT**

SPECIAL EXCERPT FROM

Read on for a sneak preview of
Just His Luck *by B.J. Daniels*.

Another scream rose in her throat as the icy water rushed in around her. She fought to free herself, but the ropes that bound her wrists to the steering wheel held tight, chafing her skin until it tore and bled. Her throat was raw from screaming, while outside the car, the wind kicked up whitecaps on the pond. The waves lapped at the windows. Inside the car, water rose around her feet, before climbing up her legs to lap at her waist.

She pleaded for help as the water began to rise up to her chest. But anyone who might have helped her was back at the high school graduation party she'd just left. If only she'd stayed at the party. If only she hadn't burned so many bridges earlier tonight. If only...

As the water lapped against her throat, she screamed even though she knew no one was coming to her rescue. Certainly not the person standing on the shore watching.

The pond was outside of town, away from everything. She knew now that was why her killer had chosen it. Worse, no one would be looking for her, not after the way she'd behaved when she'd left the party.

"You're big on torturing people," her killer had said. "Not so much fun when the shoe is on the other foot, huh?"

More than half-drunk, the bitter taste of betrayal in her mouth, she'd wanted to beg for her life. But her pride wouldn't let her. As her hands were bound to the steering wheel, she tried to convince herself that the only reason this was happening was to scare her. No one would actually kill her. Not even someone she'd bullied at school.

She was Ariel Matheson. Everyone wanted to be her friend. Everyone wanted to be her, sexy spoiled rich girl. No one hated her enough to go through with this. Even when the car had been pushed into the pond, she told herself that her new baby blue SUV wouldn't sink. Or if it did, the water wouldn't be deep enough that she'd drown.

The dank water splashed into her face. Frantic, she tried to sit up higher, but the seat belt and the rope on her wrists held her down. The car lurched under her as it wallowed almost full of water on the rough surface of the pond. Waves washed over the windshield, obscuring the lights of Whitefish, Montana, as the SUV slowly began to sink and she felt the last few minutes of her life slipping away.

She spit out a mouthful and told herself that this wasn't happening. Things like this didn't happen to her. This was not the way her life would end. It couldn't be.

Panic made her suck in another mouthful of awful-tasting water. She tried to hold her breath as she told herself that she was destined for so much more. The girl most likely to end up with everything she wanted, it said in her yearbook.

Bubbles rose around her as the car filled to the headliner, forcing her to let out the breath she'd been holding. This was real. This wasn't just to scare her.

The last thing she saw before the SUV sank the rest of the way was her killer standing on the bank in the dark night, watching her die. Would anyone miss her? Mourn her? She'd made so many enemies. Would anyone even come looking for her in the days ahead? Her parents would think that she'd run away. Her friends…

Fury replaced her fear. They thought she was a bitch before? As water filled her lungs, she swore that if she had it to do over, she'd make them all pay.

Don't miss
Just His Luck *by B.J. Daniels,*
available September 2019 wherever
Harlequin® books and ebooks are sold.

www.Harlequin.com